THE SECRETS WE KEEP

A Novel by

Britt Joni

To submit a manuscript for our review,

email us at

submissions@majorkeypublishing.com

Acknowledgments

Buddha: Thanks for being so understanding when Mommy was up so many late nights and encouraging me with your smile when I felt like giving up. You are EVERYTHING, my love, and don't you forget it. I love you more than more than most. Shoot for the stars, and reach the moon.

Mommy: YOU ARE THE TRUTH! THANK YOU FOR THE COUNTLESS THINGS YOU DO! You've been my voice of reason and my pillar of strength on days when I'm unsure of what God is trying to tell me and where He is leading me to go.

To my Big girls: Mama Britt loves y'all. You've made these last ten years so sweet. But you can't read this book until you're thirty. Lol

Jil: Thank you for kicking me in gear and encouraging me to follow my dreams. Thanks for taking the time to read when no one else would and keeping it a secret. I could never repay you for the strength you poured into me to do this.

Jess: My Jess the Mess, thanks for holding me accountable and sending me all the visuals a girl could want. You went hard for me to finish this, and I appreciate it.

Quiana: Thank you for believing in me and calming my nerves during the process of completing this novel. You could never begin to understand the magnitude of how much I appreciate you taking a chance on me.

MKP Fam: I am amazed at all of the talent I see in our group, and I am so honored to be amongst such great authors/people. Let's keep rising to the top using our dope ass pens. Thank you for welcoming me!

To the indie authors I admire: THANK YOU for lighting a spark of fire under me. Through all of your groups, I found my voice and my pen.

Sabrina: Thanks for every share and every single laugh. I'm beyond grateful for your support. As a fan, I cannot wait until the next book from The Bricks (shameless plug) is out. Don't ever put that pen down.

Nicole Falls aka Nicyonce: Thank you for unknowingly being the third link in the chain to tell me to push this pen. Thank you for the shares and for having a newbie like myself on #fallsonlove. You make my life on the internet FUN! Like legit bust your gut fun! Because of you, I am living for the day I can have a true BIWO moment. Lol

B. Love: I am grateful for you for so many things, but encouragement is what I am most thankful for. You have listened to me vent along this journey and pointed me in the right direction to get this show on the road. There were so many times that I wanted to give up, but your gentle voice of reason made me continue on. You are so right; I should never put my dreams aside because, well, life happens. You are so humble and so sweet. I don't know where you found the time to listen to my frustrations, but you did, and I am forever grateful for that.

To my family and friends: I love y'all! This year started off rough, but by the grace of God, we are still standing. Thanks for your continued support.

britt joni

-PENNING LOVE NATURALLY-

Gaea

When something feels off in your gut, it behooves you to follow that gem that's called intuition. But yet again, I'm not one to follow logic. I suppress it to appear strong when, inside, I'm letting my need to be strong yet docile and submissive drown me. I ask myself, when is enough going to be enough? When will the love I give so freely be returned? I have not one single, solitary clue as to when I'm going to put my heart first, but I know that I need to.

I can't begin to explain the countless hours I've meditated and prayed for an answer. But maybe my calls to God are going straight to a voicemail he rarely checks, because again, *nothing*. The proof of that is in the current events of today. I ignore logic, I ignore my gut, and I ignore facts. Here I am, yet again risking my freedom because this motherfucker can't stop fucking random ass bitches that somehow always bring their atrocity of a mess to my doorstep. My anger is going to get the best of me one day, but unfortunately, today won't be it. I've taken so much shit that the only logical thing I can do is evoke some of the same pain my heart keeps getting slapped with. I am—

in all essence of the word—tired.

"Gaea, come on, boo. You need to talk to me and listen to reason."

"Nah, not right now, Ana," I say to my sister, Anais, as I finish lacing up my shoes. I make quick work of getting everything I know I'm gonna need.

"Gaea, at least let me know what made your mood shift so suddenly."

I motion toward my phone as I adjust my curly pineapple ponytail and make my way back to my closet.

"*Hi, Gaea I found something that may belong to you,*" the text reads, along with a picture of my stupid ass boyfriend with his head in the naked bosom of his latest flavor of the week. I shouldn't even be mad; I'm honestly used to this type of shit. But now the bitch is texting me. There's only so much disrespect one person can take before they snap the hell out. Unfortunately, I am at that point.

"Oh, fuck no! I'll drive!" Ana shouts and grabs her keys after tossing my phone back at me.

I smirk and grab the box that I've put together. My

sister is always down to ride, even after she's instructed me to be cautious with my heart. That's Anais for you. I never understood how we came from the same household, but we're such polar opposites. Whereas I'm highly emotional and borderline insecure, she's everything but. Standing at five feet six, Anais is beautiful, and she owns it. Her body is sick. She's what most consider a BBW with a tiny waist. But her face is what draws you in. Her skin is a smooth mocha with her almond-shaped hazel eyes, a cute button nose, modestly plump lips, and a wild curly mane that's a beautiful mixture of teal, purple, and pink. I guess Ana's instinct to protect me is deeply rooted in the hurt she carries from a man she never wants to talk about, but then again, that shit could carry over from the shit our mother does.

"OK, Ana, but stay your crazy ass in the car!"

It takes us ten minutes to get to our destination. Before Ana can even put the car in park, I'm out on foot. I pour the contents of the box out, drench it in lighter fluid, and light a match. I see his precious little black-on-black BMW and pop three tires, cut up the leather seats, and shatter all but one glass because I'm nice like that. After I smirk at my handiwork, I use my key and enter his home that is soon to be ours in a matter of weeks. I take a deep breath and push forward. I'm questioning my sanity because I'm eerily calm. I sigh and kick the bedroom door in. Aaron jumps up first, while home girl screams.

"No, bitch, don't scream now! You invited me to this party, remember?"

"Bitch, you did what!" Aaron growls.

"Baby, I just thought the hoe should know we were moving forward with our family."

I raise an eyebrow. "Family, huh?" I laugh and open my purse as Aaron puts on some pants. I cock my gun and shoot off a round at him. He screams, and the bitch that's lying next to him cowers down in the fetal position.

"Get the fuck up, Aaron! I only shot you with a bean bag round!" He pats down his body, making sure that everything is intact. Hell, makes me wish it had been a real round; fucking dick-head bastard was lucky.

"You shot me! You. Really. Fucking. Shot. Me," he said, seemingly baffled. "It's not even what it seems, baby. But you... Ooooohhh, you have lost your mind!"

"Yoooo, shut up before she kills us both!"

I chuckle, surprising even myself. "What the hell do you mean, Yasmin? You're the reason she's even here! If I live through this, you're going to regret dialing her number!" Aaron roars out.

I clear my throat because, at this point, I'm tired of them talking. If I stand here any longer, the bile stuck in my throat will surely be on the floor.

"Aaron, be glad that I cherish your life more than you've ever cherished me and my love!" I growled out, swallowing my tears.

"As for you, bitch," I say as I walk over to her and put my finger in the center of her forehead. "Let this be a lesson to not invite any ol' body to your shit show of a party. In case you haven't noticed, I'm not for play. When you send for me, I'll always come bearing gifts!"

"I'm—"

I stop her because I honestly have heard enough of what she has to say. I've seen all I can stomach, and I legit feel heavy. I need to get far away from here.

I can't believe I've allowed him to bring me to this low

of a place. For years, I've prided myself on turning the other cheek. It isn't Yasmin's fault I'm here. This fault rests on the shoulders of Aaron and me. We dug the trenches and filled it with bullshit. Now the shit stinks and oozes out into our lives for others to smell as well. There's no longer a need to cover it up; it's out. Even a blind man can see the dysfunction we affectionately call us. It's a horrible representation of love, but it's unequivocally ours.

"Babe, are you going to throw away all that we've invested in this over a misunderstanding?"

"Aaron, you can't seriously be asking me that! What you need to be thanking your lucky stars for is that I haven't felt the need to shoot your dick off!"

"We can get through this."

Is this nigga serious? Like who and what the fuck does he think I am?

"We can't do—" Before I can finish my sentence, I see Ana throw punches in quick succession super close to my face.

"Now you have to be the dumbest hoe ever! She may not whoop yo' raggedy ass, but I will! I have nothing to lose!" Ana barks out. "Word to the wise, never try to sneak a bitch without first checking your surroundings!"

"Anais, I told you to stay in the damn car!"

She sucks her teeth and says, "Butterfly, put the gun away, and let's get the hell up out of here. I can't believe I left you—" I hold my hand up to stop the rant forming on her lips.

I turn to leave without a backward glance. I'm angry because I've placed my heart in Aaron's hands continuously, knowing he can't properly care for it. If I'm completely honest, I know better. He can't take care of his own heart, so how can he possibly nurture and care for mine? How foolish can one person be?

"I'll be quiet until we get to your house. There will be no I told you so's, but I'll be damned if I let you sit around and mope," Ana says as we enter her car, ignoring the crowd that has formed.

"Just get me out of here."

"Will do. But you are gonna jump that ass into something sexy and drink until you can't feel your face or remember the bastard's name!"

I silently laugh because if I know nothing else of my sister, I know she's dead ass serious.

Aaron

Gaea's ass is as crazy as sin, but I guess dealing with a nigga like me will drive you to that point in life—questioning your sanity and then coming back so that I can fuck you back into your right mind. I just never imagined my sweet little woman to roll up on me with a God damn gun. Not to mention her psycho ass shot me. I'm gonna be completely honest and say I didn't see that shit coming, even when I saw the gun. Now her sister, Anais, yeah. I would've bet money she would shoot a nigga, but not my sweet ass Gaea. She's everything that's right in this world—my angel in disguise of sorts.

But I mean, I'm a catch. I mean that in the most non-convoluted way. The shit is a hard-core fact. I'm young, handsome, and standing in line to inherit half of $10.4 million. Not to mention that upon graduation, I'll be on the board of my father's tech company, making six figures to start off. I mean, who wouldn't want me? The amount of pussy I find in my lap on a daily basis is enough to drive a saint to drink. You best believe I take advantage of that shit too. You only get one life, so why not get what I can out of it? Don't get me wrong; I love Gaea, and I'm not just talking that superficial love. I mean, I feel the shit in my soul. There's no mistaking she's my heart. Gaea is it for me, always has been. I've been lost in her world since we were fifteen years old.

You see, her father, Theodore, was brought in to handle my family's estate—and my pop's fuck ups. Typically, Theodore would only take on high-profile Civil Rights' cases. But as a favor to my pops, and his frat brother, Jeffery Williamson, he dabbled in our affairs, mostly Jeffery's. With the way Jeffery ran through women, he needed all the help he could get because simply put, my mother, Maxine, did not play. She allowed him to play around as long as he didn't make her look foolish in the process or bring any outside children home in the process. Ashlynn and I were it when it came down to the Williamson clan.

But low and behold, Jeffery fucked around with a dumb duck that was claiming pregnancy and trying to blackmail him. Pitiful thing for her because Jeffery had undergone a vasectomy upon the fifth month of my mother's pregnancy with Ashlynn. What turned out to be a terrible situation for my parents turned out to be the greatest day of my life. Theodore came rushing over with his daughters in tow.

As much as I hate to admit it, Anais caught my attention first. She was looking fine as fuck in her all black leotards. I mean, baby girl was thicker than molasses trying to be sucked through a straw. At seventeen, she was putting grown women to shame with no problems, and she knew that shit too. She came bursting through the door, attitude on full display, mumbling something about this cutting into her time with her dance coach. Seeing her get mouthy with her dad did something to me. I licked my lips and adjusted myself just as Theodore walked off, and she looked up at me. It was clear she didn't take too kindly to me staring at her ass.

"Not gonna happen, playboy. I am definitely not your speed. Yo' young ass better direct that thirsty shit on over to Butterfly!" she spat out in a whisper.

Who the fuck was Butterfly?

"First off, girl, watch ya mouth in the crib. I'm sure Mr.

20

Lee wouldn't want his princess speaking to anyone in that manner," I stated, but before I could finish, she walked up on me and cut me off, pointing her finger in my chest

"I'm far from anyone's princess! I'm pretty sure my daddy wouldn't like the fact that you are eye fucking his daughter and attempting to hide a hard dick by just a glance of all this ass. Being that I don't fuck children, he has absolutely nothing to worry about. So again, I state Butterfly is more your speed!" she spat out as she glided right past me and went sashaying down the hall to the kitchen.

I couldn't gather the rest of my thoughts to fully curse her arrogant ass out the way I wanted to. How dare she call my bluff in my own damn house? I mean, granted, she was right for a brief second. But as soon as she opened her mouth, that deadened anything I could've possibly felt for her. Instead of sitting around her ass, I headed out to meet my boy Mitchell at the park.

As I was making my way into the foyer, I heard this beautiful voice coming from our family sitting room.

Silly of me to think that you

Could ever really want me too
How I love you
You're just a lover out to score
I know that I should be looking for more
What could it be in you I see
What could it be
Oh... oh... oh... love, oh, love
Stop making a fool of me

Like a man caught in the thickest of quicksand, or more like drying cement, I was stuck in one spot, completely lost in a trance. What I may have thought I felt physically for Ana was all but forgotten. This little butterfly with a powerful voice touched my little teenage heart, and it didn't hurt that she was beautiful. She wore a modest peasant dress, paired with gladiator sandals, topped off with yellow fingernail polish on her hands and feet, and a sunflower headband laying on a cascade of long, flowy curls. I was so deep in a trance that I didn't even realize that she had stopped singing.

"Oh my goodness. I didn't think anyone else was in here. Was I loud? If so, I do apologize. Sometimes, I just get carried away," she stumbled out. Realizing that I wasn't saying anything, she continued on. "Oooookay... I'm Gaea, but most people call me Butterfly." She extended her hand out to shake.

"Nice to meet you, Gaea. I'm Aaron. You have a beautiful voice, unlike that Pitbull of a sister you have there," I finally forced out, grasping her small delicate hand, and I was rewarded with a bashful blush.

"Thanks. Don't let Ana bother you. She's just mad about Daddy having to cut her private lessons short to be a superhero to your dad."

"You heard that?" I asked as she peaked one of her eyebrows.

"No, I don't make it a habit of eavesdropping on other's conversations. But whatever she said, I'm certain she meant no harm."

And just like that, all thoughts of Mitchell were forgotten as I spent the afternoon falling for my petite queen with the big ol' voice. My Gaea. My goddess of the earth.

"So babe, now that your whore is out of the way, we

can be together," Yasmin says, bringing me back to the present day.

"Bitch, what the fuck are you even doing still being here? There will never be an us! Gaea and I will *always* be a thing!" I yell out.

Before I can toss her her clothing, Yasmin takes all her strength and punches me in the mouth. She closes her eyes and counts to twenty as I check to see if she had split my lip. After calming herself down and starting to redress, she tosses some papers on the bed, confirming that she's indeed pregnant. Ain't this some shit? I'm about to be a father, and it isn't with the person I know I'm destined to be with. Like, if anyone is carrying my seed, it should at least be Gaea.

It isn't lost on me that Yasmin is all of a sudden pregnant. I told her months back that we had to end this shit. But she keeps coming back, and I keep letting her. I mean, she isn't the only one in rotation, but hell, she does this little tongue thing that makes sure she's in my line-up. She's had her eye on me since I first stepped foot on this campus. Only problem was I wasn't checking for that

Southern Belle act. Yeah, she's fine and stupid dumb thick, but I'm not about to chase her when I have Gaea. All I want is to occasionally fuck her; I'm not trying to be her man. Nah, I'm super good on that. Gaea is everything she isn't, and if this shit turns out to be true, confirmation be damned, then I may lose her forever. I know what has to be done.

"Get rid of it!" I roared out.

"I figured you would say some slick shit like that. As luck would have it, it's already too late. You and I, sir, are stuck together. So you probably should get used to the idea of having me around."

Muthafuck me! This bitch trapped me! Judging from the smug look on her face, she thinks she has won this round. Too bad for her—my parents, but especially Maxine Williamson, didn't raise a fool. We aren't for play. After snatching her purse out of the chair, she bounces toward the door in triumph. Seeing red, I pop her celebratory balloon.

"I want a paternity test. There is no telling how many niggas you were fucking. If it comes back being mine," I half-sneer, half-chuckle. "You better be ready for the fight of your life because I am coming for full custody!"

I don't even give her time to react before I slam the door. I stalk over to my bar to pour myself a drink before I make the dreaded phone call to Maxine. She warned me that my continuing to fuck off was going to ruin our plans. But I thought I was invincible. Hell, in many senses of the word, I am. I'm the golden boy, but moms isn't about to go for that. She's going to eat me alive, and Janet! My God, Janet! Her evil ass is gonna cook me to serve to my mother. I pick up the phone and dial my mother.

"Hello. Aaron? I really don't have time to talk right now; Janet and I are on our way to meet with a caterer, so make it fast."

"Aye, Ma. You may want to cool things down with the caterer and shit. I fucked up bad with Gaea. I need you and Mrs. Janet to help me fix this."

"Did you just curse me? If I were near you, I'd slap your damn face off! What the hell do you mean, you messed things up with Gaea?" she spat out

Hearing Gaea's name, her mother immediately

snatches the phone and asks me to explain everything that has transpired. After being called everything but a child of God, we all formulate a plan to get Gaea back. I just pray that God will show me some leniency and bring my baby back. But until then, I wait.

Gaea

The amount of alcohol my girls and I have consumed since leaving Aaron's house is enough to make an alcoholic blush. My bestie, Jenn, has also joined in on this celebration of sorts—a celebration of almost a decade of heartache. Mine, at that. I guess that's the running theme. I won't sit here and put on this big, brave front like I'm not hurting. Because no lie, I'm drowning in that hurt.

I gave that fool seven years of my life. Seven fucking years I can't get back. If it had not been for Jenn and Ana, I would be in a corner somewhere, balled up, crying, and licking my wounds. But I made the conscious decision to no longer cry over someone who is continuously abusing my heart. Aaron is so fucking disrespectful with his shit that it isn't funny. I honestly can't say I expected any different from him. I mean, look who he had as an example to lead him as a man. Every ounce of what he has done to me is a direct result of some shit he's learned while growing up. But foolishly, I choose to look past that and let him wreak havoc on my heart for years. He wasn't always this way, though.

In the beginning, Aaron was so dope. Like, he was legit, I don't know... different. He wasn't like the other guys that were sniffing around Ana and me. Well, mostly Ana because my sister's the shit, and I'm literally just her little sister. But Aaron saw through that. He saw my heart—or so I would like to believe that's what he saw. I mean, his real fine ass would stumble over words during our first interactions. It was so bad that some days when we were together, we would sit in a comfortable silence. He would just flash his gorgeous smile, and I would just sing, using the melody to have a conversation with his heart. We used the worst summer in his parents' marriage and became super tight. My dad was putting out a fire, and I was kicking it with Aaron.

Truthfully, at first, I wasn't checking for him on some relationship type shit. I liked him, but I knew his type— too handsome for his own good, rich, super athletic, a Jack and Jill prototype, an expensive ass prep school scholar, and charming to boot. Not to mention the fact that when my mother discovered he was truly into me, she began to adore him, which, if I'm completely honest, was a strike in the wrong direction. Janet had a way of turning sugar to shit. Something so blissfully perfect would crumble in her hands.

I intended to only be friends with Aaron, but somehow, that friendship blossomed into more. He became my sunshine when my mother was being intolerable, and I became his refuge when he was sinking into his parents' shit. He understood that I used music to escape; it kept me mellow and sane. In turn, I understood the guy behind the gorgeous smile that wanted to be a better man than his father. We were the balance each of us needed to get through our days.

We were so tight until, one day, we just weren't. I was only seventeen and still very much innocent when I received my first 'I'm coming to you as a woman' call. I was so shaken; I didn't know what to do besides hang up. Oh, but Anais did! She pulled down on that girl so fast and made me confront her. She explained to me that the moment I allowed her to disrespect me, I was setting the tone to allow her to continue. Needless to say, Ana was wrong, but I wouldn't dare tell her that. The dirty games that she played only quadrupled once she got a response. That warped way of thinking is what led me to me always fighting bitches. My petite, always in a sunny disposition ass was really going to war over a man—well, really boy— that was supposed to be mine.

Aaron, by all means, was remorseful. Well, as remorseful as getting caught up would get, but hey, I had to take what he was giving, right? Right. He did good for about a year without drama unfolding. No girls or anything as far as I knew. He was all about me, all about us, with the progression of building an empire. We were all set for the both of us to go to Brown State. He would be studying engineering, and I would be studying nursing. We had a fool-proof plan, and I was for sure I would be Mrs. Aaron Williamson.

I remember my twenty-first birthday. Aaron worked so hard to make it special. We flew out to Vegas with a couple of our friends and turned the hell up. I mean, bottle popping all night, suites for our young asses, and club hopping. Being that I was newly twenty-one, I wanted to gamble, and not just with little money—I mean *gamble*. I just wanted to see what it was like and see if I would actually like it. Low and behold, I sat my ass down at the Blackjack table to play, and I was winning. When I say winning, I mean I was up to like $25,000 when I only started with one thousand. Talk about beginner's luck. Before I had time to even grasp what was happening, I lost it. I lost it all. Unlike Ana and Jenn's ass, Aaron didn't make me feel bad about it. He kissed my forehead, grabbed my hand, and led me out of the casino. He assured me that everything was going to be OK and never spoke a word on it again.

We walked hand-in-hand down the strip until we stumbled into a liquor store. We grabbed the biggest bottles of Patron and Hennessy and headed back to our suite. While I settled in in front of the TV, getting lost in one of my favorite feel-good movies—*Grease*—Aaron disappeared in the bathroom. Shortly after making it halfway through *Hopelessly Devoted to You*, I was summoned to the bathroom. Upon entering the bathroom, I saw that he had run my bath and added all of my favorite essential oils. As I stood in shock, he began to undress me, and he led me to the tub. Once I began to soak in the bath, he eased in behind me and started to gently massage my scalp.

"You know, Gaea, being here with you right now means everything to me. I foresee us being at this for a lifetime," he assured me.

"Aww, babe, that's so sweet. I can't wait until the day that I am yours forever. Thanks so much for not making me feel so bad about today," I murmured.

"Don't mention it, boo. You know I love me some you," he said as he turned me around to straddle him. He pulled my lips to his and brought his thumb to my now throbbing bud. Aaron strummed on my sweet spot as if he were a world-renowned violinist, giving me my first orgasm within minutes. After giving me a few moments to settle down, he placed a kiss on my forehead and whispered, "I want you, my love. I want to bind our souls for the rest of our lives. Will you let me?"

Completely lost in his trance, I gave my most prized possession to him willingly, thoroughly, thinking I was securing a future with him. Oh, how deliciously flawed that thinking was. But Aaron was gentle. He drained the tub and scooped me up. He slowly walked us over to the bed. Once he laid me down on the bed, he placed soft kisses from the crown of my head down to the teal polish on my toes. He gently began to work his way up from my toes to my sweet spot. He placed soft kisses on my lips before he gave slow licks to my clitoris, sending warm sensations to every nerve ending in my body.

Just as I thought he had done enough, he suckled my bud into his mouth, and the muthafuckin' hums made me bring my hands down to his head and pull him deeper into my pussy. What did I do that for? He went off, sending me wave for wave into orgasmic bliss, damn near blinding me. My baby was putting in work, staking his claim on my body and me. After he waited until I landed from my flight, he gave me the sloppiest of kisses, sending my yoni into overdrive.

"Can I make love to you now, babe?" he asked as he pulled a condom out of the bedside table. I nodded my head in agreeance, unable to form the words with my mouth quite yet. As nervous as I was, I knew this was what I needed to do to secure our future. Yeah, again, flawed thinking—flawed like a muthafucka—but in that moment, all I cared about was connecting with my man on a spiritual level.

Before I had the chance to formulate my next thought, I felt a delicious amount of pressure invading my sweet spot. Aaron used his fingers to stimulate my clitoris and his tongue to play around with my taut nipples to distract me from the pain. When he had fully invaded my love canal, he went still for a moment to allow me time to adjust to the fit of him. And boy was it a good amount to feel and adjust to. My baby was blessed.

After a few moments of adjusting, I wiggled, letting him know it was OK to move. Aaron slowly pulled out and dove back in. He continued this delectable pace, picking up slowly as I would let out soft moans, completely lost in the feeling and smell of us. When he lifted my legs and started to brush against my g-spot, I was hooked, lost in the feeling and wanting to hold this in my heart forever. I started to meet him pump for pump, pound for pound, beautiful stroke after beautiful stroke, driving us both into indescribable orgasmic bliss. It was so good and so sweet that my overgrown ass was shedding happy tears.

After that weekend, I knew, without a doubt, that I loved Aaron. He was supposed to be my husband. But all that I got out of the deal was a glorified fuckboy with everything in credentials that parents would want for their little girl—without the gift of honesty and monogamy.

A loud pounding on my door brought me out of thoughts.

"What inna de world?" Jenn slurs out in Jamaican Patois. Knowing that it could only be one person, I storm to the door, grabbing my gun in the process.

I swing the door open yelling, "Aaron, I am not above shooting yo' trifling ass! Stop fucking playing me for weak!" I'm stunned into silence by the sight of my mother, Janet, and Aaron's mother, Maxine. I huff, knowing this shit just can't be happening. I don't give a damn what they have to say this time around; I'm not about to be suckered into going backward again. I don't think my mother got it, but this is one of the main problems I have with her. She always puts her fucking status above family!

"Gaea, put that gun away! I didn't raise you to run

around here like some sophisticated hood rat!" my mother spits out with her nose turned up as if something stunk. I just stand there, looking at her with an equally disgusted look on my face.

"Mother, if you're coming over here to convince Butterfly to go back to Aaron, I am calling Daddy! Enough is enough already! Put your God damn daughter before a fucking legacy!" Ana spits out.

"Ana, I hardly see how this is any of your business at all. You clearly wouldn't understand the importance of this, given your current occupation! Giving up Yale!" Maxine said, looking down her nose at my sister. I look at my mother, pleading with her in my mind to stand up for her daughter. But of course, she finds more interest in her nails than her children. Fucking bitch. I can't wait to talk to my daddy about the piece of shit he married. This shit sobers me up real fast.

"First of all, Mrs. Maxine, don't address me—like, at all. I'm in my right mind to slap you for all of the hundreds of mistresses you allow your husband to have. Second, what decision I may or may not have made is none of your fucking business. Am I asking anybody is this fucking room to support me? No. So for you to speak on it is asking for you to get popped right in your God damn mouth! Furthermore, I'll be damned if I allow you two dimwits to turn Gaea into Maxine!" Ana snarls out.

"Ana, let me handle them!" I scream. It's evident that this shit is getting out of control. What I don't need is for Ana to fight this battle for me. I'm more than capable of standing up for myself. Hell, I am not weak by any means. Gullible maybe, but weak no. Theodore didn't raise a punk. If he knew half the shit I've put up with, family ties be damned; he would put Aaron through a wall and shut his wife the fuck up for once. But no, I'm still searching for a love from a mother who put a legacy before the children she's birthed. That's some sick and twisted shit—love that's conditional on what and where we can land her on the status. But that's my mother for you, pushing an agenda instead of parenting.

"Ana, Gaea, I'm gonna head out. I'll hit you all up if I decide to venture out later," Jenn states before rushing to the door, past my mother and Maxine

"Ana, I wouldn't expect you to understand what it's like to have someone from a good home to want to build a future with you!" Maxine spits out. At that moment, I still don't know why I'm expecting Janet to check Maxine for being so clearly out of line and speaking to her Ana that way. But I am, and the shit is foul. All this wench has to do to is shut Maxine up with a few simple but stern words, but nope. Her ass is still over there playing with her stupid ass nails. That infuriates me. Like, bitch, we came from your womb.

"A good home? Bitch, please! Let me call my daddy, because it's obvious that Janet's ass is off her fucking meds to barge up in here and allow your two-bit polyester-wearing, bad-weave-having ass to talk to me as if you both aren't pushing Gaea to be with Aaron for your own selfish gain!" Ana yells as she begins to call our daddy. The look on those two witches' faces is priceless. They know Theodore doesn't bullshit when it comes down to his girls. While he loves our mother, he doesn't put up with her shit when it comes down to his girls.

"You know, Mother, I don't know why I expected

more out of you, but I did. How dare you let someone speak to your own flesh and blood like that. Like, damn, you act as if you hate your own daughter. Maybe you do, but I'll be damned if I allow anyone to disrespect her in my presence in my home! Which leads me to you, Maxine! Don't ever fix your mouth to disrespect my sister when you've done a half ass job in raising your son. There is absolutely nothing you two can say to make me get back with Aaron. That situation is dead. Read my lips: D-E-A-D! What Maxine should be worrying about is the damn child he created with some yamp while he was supposed to be loving and preparing for a life with me! Now what I need for the both of you to do is get the fuck up out of my house! I have plans with my sister!"

Stunned into silence, Maxine begins to collect her things as my mother struggles to find her words—words that I no longer care to hear. It's too little too late. Anything she has to say at this point won't be received well.

"This isn't over, Gaea. You and Aaron both will work this out. Whether it be by force or choice!" Maxine snarls out. "Now I love you as if you were my very own child, and I would hate to lose what we've grown to have due to a simple misunderstanding. This situation between Aaron and his common whore can be fixed; I'm almost sure of it. Take some time to think about your future. Give me a call once you've thought over it and are done being mad."

"Maxine, I love you and your son as well, but at some point, you have to love you more than you love a man and more than you love any wealth you may encounter. Unfortunately, or fortunately enough for me, I've reached that point. I have to love me more and love Aaron from a distance," I say, and she lets out this dramatic ass huff and storms toward the front door. As my mother stands to approach me, I shake my head, signaling there's nothing I need her to say. Her moment to be a mother has come and gone. She sucks up her unshed tears, and they both head out of my apartment, not making it far before my father greets them.

"Well, hello there, Maxine. There is a lot I would like to say to you, but I can't, because you are a woman—a woman that has no ties to me—so I won't address you, but be sure to let your husband know he should be expecting a call from me by nights' end. A word to the wise that I need you and Janet both to understand. Those two girls in that condo behind you, I'd lose my mind and go to war behind them," he says all calm and smooth. "Janet, say goodnight. We have some business to take care of."

As my father makes his way into my condo, I feel a sense of peace I can't find the words to describe. It makes me forget about the bullshit from earlier in the day. I feel safe and loved. The only other time I ever felt this type of peace, I was hanging with my homie Kwame. He allowed me to be unapologetically me. I mean, like Aaron did in the beginning, before his mother and my mother had him believing I was his for sure. Man, fuck Aaron. As soon as I see Kwame, I am no longer going to fight the attraction I feel for him. I am going to let that shit be known.

"Hey, sweetheart. Where is your sister?" my daddy asks, pulling me into a hug and kissing my forehead.

"I'm right here, Daddy," Ana announces, putting on her fake ass, innocent daughter act, kissing him on his cheek. I giggle a little bit, but I'm not gonna blow up her spot. I'll let her live this time. "So where is Mad ass Max?"

"Really, Ana?" I asked. "Her and Ma are outside bu—
" Before I could finish, Ana ran out of the door. My father and I race behind her. By the time we made it outside, Ana was pulling Maxine back out of her car by her hair, sending pieces of raggedy ass weave flying across the lawn.

"Bitch you were talking all that shit before don't think that I was going to let yo ass leave before beating that ass!" Ana screamed out as she threw a series of blows to her torso. Maxine was so shook up she started wind milling. That windmill was no match for Ana, she took the opportunity of Maxine losing her footing and ended up on top of her landing a series of hits to her face and torso. "I told yo old ass to stop fucking with me! I told you to mind your fucking business, but no you had to open yo raggedy ass mouth to try to down talk somebody like yo husband hasn't been trying to get a whiff of this pussy since it became legal!"

"Ana stop it's not worth it!" I yelled

"Anais Lee I raised you better than this. Stop this foolishness at once!" Janet screeched as we watched the two women rolling all throughout the grass tussling.

"You lying ass slut" Maxine yelled finding her strength from somewhere to toss Ana off "What would my husband want with common pussy when he has a pussy wrapped in gold at home?"

"Bitch tell that lie to a young bitch that actually wants ya bum ass husband" Ana said as Maxine delivered a slap to her cheek.

"That's enough!" My father roared! "Ana take yo ass in the house and Maxine get back in your car and leave!" Ana looked at our father appearing to take in what he said nodded once and begin walking towards the house. As if she thought about the last slap she turned around and delivered two punches to Maxine's jaw and nose. I could hear the bones cracking from the impact sending blood spurting everywhere.

"Let that be a lesson to watch who the fuck you are talking to" Ana spat out as she walked calmly to my door. Janet just sat there looking dumb as usual and our pour father was stunned into disbelief. Never would we have imagined that Ana would react this way in regards to these two women but I guess with the amount of alcohol we had consumed and the amount of anger she had inside it was a shit show waiting to happen.

"Janet clean this up with Maxine and pay her whatever we need to get her jaw and nose fixed. But I trust this will be kept silent." He said as he stormed off to

As we wait for my mother to enter the condo, I give him a quick run-down of my life with Aaron. The more I speak, the more perplexed he looks. I feel terrible because as long as I've been alive, Theodore Lee has been my protector, provider, and if parents could truly ever be your friends, he's been just that.

"Butterfly, I think I've heard enough. If I am to hear anymore, I don't think I'd ever be able to face that boy, his family, or your mother. But I will say this; you deserve so much more than what Aaron could ever offer you." As my door opens, he lifts his eyes toward it, looking directly at my mother. "I love you, Janet, but I will not tolerate you disrespecting our daughter. I don't allow them to disrespect you, so I'll be damned if I continue to allow you to walk all over them."

"Honey, I was only—" my mother began, only to be

cut off.

"You was only about to find yourself without a family. Yeah, they are grown, but these are my babies. Hell, your babies. Act like you give a fuck about them. Any of us for that matter. Our first priority as their parents is to protect them, not letting other people walk all over them. The next time I hear you've allowed any of your uppity ass friends to disrespect any child of mine, you will live to regret it," my father states matter-of-factly. "Here, girls. Your night out will be funded by your mother."

After he closes the door, Ana begins to jump around all excitedly, while I sit and write down a poem that won't get out of my head.

There is a struggle in loving you.
I'm not speaking on the beauty of love.
The oh my God, there goes my baby kinda love.
The my word is my bond kinda love.
The this is a forever type of love.
The I trust you with my peace and light kinda love.
No baby I don't get that type of love.
The struggle in loving you is

Lies…

Resentment…

Uncertainty…

Emptiness…

Soaking in regret…

My heart I can no longer neglect

The love I get is a thin line between love and hate kinda love.

A this motherfucker is psychotic type of love.

This bastard is gonna make me put my foot on his neck kinda love.

How could I have ever been so stupid? Kinda love.

My brain is all scattered, no longer willing to explain the feelings I keep sheltered.

The silent battle I keep at bay.

It's difficult to bury feelings when they all have names

Meghan,

Tiffany,

Cassandra,

and I'm sure there's a couple of Becky's

Running off all of these names is damn sure

reminiscent of DMX's "What These Bitches Want"

Instead of fighting for what I know I deserve

Instead of putting my foot on your throat

I smile and bite my cheek

While continuing to crash, waiting for the burn.

This motherfucker thinks I'm weak, a hand game of sorts.

Baby boy better realize this round of spades is about to get his ass cut.

This shit's getting too deep, my emotions a literal bomb.

I sit...

I watch...

and I plot how to hit you where it burns...

I'm throwing a match

I'm igniting a flame; hopefully you'll regret the day you ever asked me my name.

There is no return from the scars you've caused.

There's no evidence of the pain you've inflicted.

Those tears I've cried are only a fading memory.

I know exactly where to hit you, your weakness of

course.

While you're diving in that canal

I'm silently watching and waiting

I take a sip of my Henny

I swallow all my grief

Feet, don't fail me now

Courage, don't neglect me.

I hear you

I feel you

What part of that don't you get?

This is my moment

I know you're vulnerable just like me

I watch you spill your seeds in a body that surely doesn't matter.

I wonder if you both realize that I've entered the room

I smile as I aim and let off my rounds.

Two to the heart, and one to the brain.

The look on your face as your pleasure turned into pain

Will be one I cherish in honor of your name.

Maybe in your next life, you'll realize my love for you was never a game.

Feeling my buzz wear off, I hustle in my room to get dressed, all the while thinking that tonight will be a great night for me because, well, I planned it that way.

Kwame

I don't know how often I must say the club scene is just not my thing anymore. It used to be flattering to go out and have these beautiful women literally throwing more pussy in my lap than I could fathom. But after a while, that shit gets old. I started to notice it's not me they're after; I'm just a bonus. Women see me, and dollar signs appear. I can pinpoint when Kwame Langston Jacobsen becomes dollars, euros, and pesos. I would always break hearts when it became evident that none of them had a chance at my wallet, nor did they have a chance at me. I can only offer them one night, and after that, I'm done. My main focus is getting my mom and little sister out of the hood. That's been my goal since I picked up a ball. That and obtaining a degree that I can use long after I've surpassed my glory days with balling.

Maybe my plan stems from the fact I want to break through the stereotypes placed upon me by a nation that systematically wants me to fail. Even as a young cat, it was never lost on me growing up that I had four strikes against me. I was born African American. I was born male. I was born poor. I was born to an African American woman who was forced into single parenthood by a man who didn't give a country fuck to be present. Well, I take that back. He became present once I started making a name for myself. Then I couldn't get rid of his ass no matter how much I would ignore him.

"Yo, Kwam! Act like you want to be in this muthafucka. Look at all these bad bitches ready to suck the skin off a nigga!" Tobias excitedly exclaimed.

"Groupies, my man! Groupies! I'm not with that tonight; I'm just here to kick it with my boys before we are all thrown into the world of sharks."

Tobias sucks his teeth, but he too is well aware of the combine we've been waiting for since we were children. I glance around Amour Noir and I must say I'm impressed with T's pick for tonight. It's about time he finally starts listening to me. This Neo-Soul/Jazz spot is a contemporary bar in appearance alone, decorated tastefully in beautiful browns and blacks with hints of teal all around. The artwork on the wall is eccentric but really subtle. I'm so into the details of the club that I'm half ass listening to

Tobias.

"Yo, Kwam! Who the fuck is that with Ana's mean ass?"

I follow his line of vision to see he's losing his mind over our homegirl Gaea. The sight of her makes my mouth go completely dry and causes me to shift the tightness straining against my pants. "Damn!" I utter as I start making my way toward her.

Gaea is nothing short of gorgeous, even without the little getup she's sporting now. Tonight, she's sex on wheels, wearing a skin-tight black midi hugging her in all the right places and enhancing areas that would otherwise go unnoticed and some sexy ass red stilettos that elongate her legs. She's bad, standing at about five feet three with a petite, athletic body with curves in all the right places, an ample ass, a cute, heart-shaped face with a button nose, plump, plush lips, and almond-shaped, coffee-colored eyes.

"I know, bro. That bitch is bad!" Tobias exclaims.

"T, mane, watch yo' mouth. That's Gaea."

"Fuck no. Gaea don't look like that."

"Well, look again because that is most definitely her."

"Aaron is one lucky, dog ass muthafucka. How did he luck up on somebody like—" He cuts his sentence short as we approach Anais and Gaea.

"Well, if it isn't the prince and his leper!" Ana says as Gaea chokes on her drink.

"Oh, Ana, look at you, looking how you looking!" a visibly irritated T replies.

"Which is bomb as fuck!" she says as she does a full 360 and wiggles her voluptuous ass in a hot-pink romper.

"Yeah, you aight. It's yo' mouth that's trifling. You need somebody to fuck that flip ass mouth out your system," he says with a smirk as Ana picks her jaw up off the ground. "What's up, Gae! How have you been?"

"Hey T, I've been—"

"Savage as fuck," Anais says, laughing her ass off as Gaea rolls her eyes and smacks her fire-engine-red lips.

"Hey, Gypsy! I've missed seeing your face in the library," I say as she smiles as she always does when I call her Gypsy. She got the nickname from me because she's the artsy type without being stereotypical; it's literally who she is. She's dressed bohemian chic with a modern spin. Her aura is chill, and she has a dope ass spirit. She always smells of sunshine, blueberries, and sunflowers. On top of all of that, she's woke. Her social consciousness in regards to African American people and their troubles systematically is a turn on for sure. What I admire the most about her is that she's a free spirit and true to herself. She's so clutch that I can't fathom why she would ever play around with a cat like Aaron.

"Hey, Sweet Pea." She giggles as she engulfs me in a hug that makes my dick hard. "It has been a while, but I doubt you missed seeing me around."

"Girl, quit playing. I hit you up on multiple occasions. I mean, you've only been my WCW since I've met you. "

"You're right, and you had all these little heffas stalking me." She let out with a loud laugh, pushing her breasts flush against me. If I'm not mistaken, I swear she's flirting with me.

"So how are you and Aaron?"

"Me and who?" she asks, releasing me from the hug I've gotten so comfortable in.

"Your dude, yo' MCM, yo' bae, your—"

"Man, fuck dude! That's a dead issue! I need another drink."

"What's up, Kwame? Ignore Butterfly. Her adrenaline has finally worn off after she went all Angela Bassett in *Waiting to Exhale* on dude ass!"

"Shut up, Ana!" Gaea growled out.

"OK, but don't shoot me too!" She cackled as she dragged Tobias to the bar. "I'm gonna make you forget Aaron's existence."

After they're a good distance away, I ask, "Would you like to talk about it?"

She shakes her head no and starts moving to a singer crooning about the number of drinks it would take to lead someone to his home. As I watch her body roll and her ass sway, I realize I'm not the only male enamored with Gaea. That thought makes my ears hot and causes my body to warm over. I can't believe this shit; I'm pissed off over someone who doesn't belong to me.

Where the fuck did that come from? I wonder. This has literally been my homie since she spilled blueberry tea all over me in an African American studies class our freshman year. Either way, I'm not about to let the next man put his hands all over her.

"Dance with me, Gaea," I demand as I take her hands and pull her body close. She places one of her luscious thighs between my legs so that we are pelvis to pelvis, and she begins a sensual slow grind. Sade's velvet voice is flowing through this club, encasing us in this world where it's just her and me. I pull her closer, meeting her beat for beat.

There's a quiet storm
And it never felt like this before
There's a quiet storm that is you
There's a quiet storm
And it never felt this hot before
Giving me something that's taboo

I don't recall a time Gaea has ever been this free with me. Always cautious, never crossing the line, keeping a strictly platonic relationship. But tonight, something is different. Just when I think my dick can't get any harder, she turns around and places her ass on my length, moving at an agonizingly slow pace. Before I can stop myself, I'm wrapping my arms around her waist and dipping my head to place kisses on her neck.

She moans a beautiful melody of lust and desire. As if she reads my mind, she whips around and locks eyes with me. In those coffee-colored eyes, I see the smoldering heat of lust, and I'm hypnotized by this beautiful woman. Unable to stop myself and vocalize my need for her, I take her mouth. I swear, as cliché as it sounds, I see stars. As Sade continues to serenade us, I feel Gaea gripping my shirt while she's placing wanton kisses on my lips.

As if on cue, the song ends, and we jump apart. Anais and Tobias are now back with our drinks. Gaea looks away, biting her lips as I pull her back in front of me to hide the erection we just created. Ana gives T a knowing look and tries to suppress a laugh. Fed up with the sexual tension, Gaea puffs her chest out, grabs my hand and says, "Kwam, let's get out of here," and leads me out of the club.

*****

I take Gaea back to my place because for whatever reason, she doesn't want to go back to hers. It's not my business, but I can't help it. I can't ignore the pain she is trying to mask behind her eyes. I glance over at her sitting on my bed and ask, "Would you like something to drink?"

"No, Kwam. I want you. I need you now."

"I'm not sure you're ready for that, babe. I can see you're hurting, and I don't want this to be something you live to regret."

"Kwam, please don't deny me. I need you to help me to take the pain away," she says as she steps out of her panties.

"Gaea, I don't—"

Before I can get my sentence out, she's climbed onto my lap, silencing me with an electrifying kiss.

I try my hardest to resist the urge, but unfortunately, it's a losing battle. I pull back. "Babe, once we cross this line, I want you to be aware that there is no turning back. I need you to understand the ramifications of what we are about to do."

"Darling, I've never been surer about anything in my life."

I swallow my better judgment and give into flesh,

despite my spirit telling me to go in the opposite direction. I feel it in my gut that nothing will be the same after this, but still, I can't stop myself. My spirit is screaming at me to feed her soul and to speak to and stroke her bleeding heart. But how can I explain to her that my soul has this innately deep desire to heal her soul, even if it were only temporary, without freaking her out? I know no other way to do this than to be completely open and direct.

"Gaea Lee, look at me," I say so that she can look up, see, and understand how serious I am. When I'm sure her almond, hazel eyes have met mine, I continue. "I can give you all of the physical pleasure your heart could ever possibly desire, but right now, in this here moment, I'm going to take my time and caress your soul and make love to your heart. If you're not prepared for that, I need you to speak up now." I see a look of confusion play across her face, so I continue. "If I can't do those things for you, then we can't continue. You're important to me, Gypsy, so if I'm going to take care of you, I have to start with your heart."

She glances back up at me and croaks out, "Just stop

talking and do whatever it is you need to do."

"God, you're beautiful," I say as I lean over to kiss her deeply, passionately. I draw my body against hers and grasp her firmly. I trace kisses along her ears, then down her neck, then down her arm and speak softly into her ear. "I'm not just talking about the things that the world can see; I'm speaking of the inner you. The beauty of your spirit beguiles me, the stillness of your soul arouses me, and the quiet strength of your heart enthuses me."

I drop my hand down, reach under the hem of her dress, and slide it along her thigh. Slowly, I move it higher and higher along her smooth skin. The edge of my hand feels the heat first, then the baldness of her sweet spot, and finally the wet oasis of her pussy. She closes her eyes and gasps, and her legs spread wider as she pushes her pussy against my hand. Seeing the pleasure play all over her face, I turn my hand ninety degrees and gently run my middle finger up and down her clitoris. I slowly push my finger into her canal and hear her breath catch. Gaea smiles a devious smile as I ease my finger in and out of her. Right when I can feel she's at her peak, I remove my fingers. I put my fingers into her mouth so she can taste herself and whisper against her lips. "You are intelligent, you are beautiful, and you are more than worthy to be loved."

After uttering those words, Gaea takes one step back and pulls the dress right over her head in record time. I wet my lips as I fall to my knees to come face to face with her pussy. I grasp the back of her thighs and pull her close and begin to gently kiss around the toffee center. Upon smelling her arousal, I run my tongue up her vagina, finding it as sweet and delicious as the most succulent peach. Gaea lays back, closes her eyes, and runs her fingers through my hair. I glance up and take a survey of how the sensations are playing across her face.

"That feels amazing," she whimpers. I gently insert two fingers into her pussy, pushing in as far as I can. Then I curve my fingers to locate then stroke her G-spot and apply pressure.

"Ahhh, Kwame!"

I can feel her nearing her peak, so I increase pressure and pinch her mouth-watering nipples. "Come on, baby. Give it to me. Come on. Give me what I'm owed." As if on cue, Gaea explodes. The dam breaks, her orgasm ripping through her entire body and soul. A deep groan emanates from her lips as a wave of incredible pleasure spreads from her pelvis down through her thighs, leaving the evidence all over my face. With her mouth open and unable to catch her breath, Gaea's entire body shudders convulsively once, twice, three times.

"Oh my God, that was inconceivable."

"Oh, baby, you haven't seen anything yet," I say as I quickly undress.

After dispensing of my clothes, I pull her into me and kiss her with everything I have inside. I need her to feel that this is more than just sex to me. I want her to feel all that my mouth won't say. I need her to know that after this, things will never be the same. She's now mine. "Gaea, once we connect on this spiritual level, I need you to know that you are mine."

"Less talking, more feeling, Kwam." She moans out as she strokes the head of my dick. I gather up her breasts in my hands and then began to lavish kisses on these mocha mounds. I suck one of her nipples into my mouth, sending shivers throughout her body. Gaea reaches down to pull my dick into her opening to tease me a little bit. I inhale sharply as I hear her say, "Put it in me. Now."

I watch as she maneuvers her body so that her ass is barely on the bed, and she pushes her pussy forward, just above my hips. I position my dick at the entrance of her very wet, very engorged pussy.

"Come on, stop teasing me." With that, I lean forward, thrusting my length deep into her. "Ohhh, yes, baby!" Gaea wails. "Oh yeah. Oh my God, that feels remarkable!"

I don't disagree. As I continue to drive in and out of her pussy, I feel each stroke get more powerful than the last. I can sense she is on the verge as well; she's showing all the tell-tale signs of her first orgasm. Our breathing becomes tattered, and our moans, deafening.

"Come on, baby," Gaea urges me. "Give it to me. Deep in me. Fuck me so good, baby."

My strokes get faster and grow more urgent. I start pounding myself against Gaea's G-spot. I feel her pussy begin to contract around me, and know I'm fighting a losing battle in trying to hold out any longer.

"Yes!" she screams as her second orgasm hits. While she's still convulsing, I let out a loud groan, emptying myself into her sweet, sweet depths. As our spasms and contractions gradually fade, I place a final kiss on her lips. I tell her, "You're perfect." I pull her close, and it feels so good to hold each other, both on the outside and the inside.

"Gaea, you have one month to wrap things up with ol' dude. After I return from the combine, I expect you to be all mine. Do we have an understanding?"

"Yes, baby, one month," she says as she straddles me, and we begin our second round of lovemaking.

Gaea

Last night was nothing short of amazing. I can't believe with a sober brain that Kwame and I have taken our friendship to the next level, completely intoxicated anyway, between the confrontation with the mothers from hell and Ana's big ass mouth. I was just buzzed, completely aware of what was going on, and to be completely honest, I loved every single sweet moment of it. Kwame and me. That has a good ring to it.

I'm excited about the possibilities of what can be. Not just potential, although it's there, but also the manner in which he made love to not only me but my heart. My God was I gonna fall for him. *Hard.* There's no doubt about that. Not that I am, but what's plaguing me is the month he has given me to end things with Aaron. What I thought was already clear and verbalized is actually incomplete, as made evident by seeing Aaron's trifling ass sitting in his car. I guess he thinks because he isn't parked in my driveway, I can't see him. What did I ever see in his ass? Swallowing my disgust for him, I get out of my vehicle and head toward my door.

"Where the fuck have you been, Butterfly? I've been waiting out here all night! I'd expect this shit from yo' hoe ass sister, but you? Nah!" he hisses out.

"Look, Aaron, I thought I made shit clear with you yesterday. I. Do. Not. Want. You! I'm good on you. This shit between us is done. Let me say this again so that you can get this through your head. I. Do. Not. Want. You! Like it's legit all bad. That point is further driven into the ground by you putting your mouth on my sister. She had nothing to do with us—specifically you fucking all these bitches. I don't give a fuck what who says; I will not budge on this. Save your mother a trip and a phone call and let it go. I'm firm on that!" I say as I try to walk off.

Imagine my surprise when he grabs ahold to my arm and won't let go. It's clear that he's lost his mind. There's no logical reason other than that. In all the years we've been together, he never has so much as touched me other than with a loving hand. Looking over him now, he looks disheveled. His eyes are bloodshot red, and his body is tense. Yeah, he's not the Aaron I knew, but nothing excuses his putting his hands on me. That's a hard no; I don't care what you're going through.

"Butterfly, I get that you are mad. But what we are not gonna do is to pretend as if we are done. I'm yours, and you are mine. You about to let some yamp ass slut destroy what we built. Nah, it ain't going down like that. What you are gonna do is go in that damn house, pack your shit, and continue on as planned."

I go to snatch my arm away, and he squeezes. I'm not with this fuck shit, so I go in my bag and pull my mace. Securing it in my palm, I wait and shift my body to completely face him.

"Have you lost your damn mind? Get your hands off of me not now, but right fucking now!" I say as I try to yank my arm away, but this nigga has the nerve to squeeze tighter. I take my mace, spray his ass dead in his eyes, and punch him dead in the nose. I don't know what part of I'm not for play that he doesn't comprehend to make him try me again, but I'm more than happy to show him. Punk ass! As he screams and hollers, holding his bloody nose and trying to wipe at his burning eyes, I walk right over his ass and head right into my house, slamming my door behind me. He has me so super fucked up that it isn't funny. He let this sunny disposition overshadow that on some days, I was Hennessy on the rocks, mixed with a pack of Newport shorts.

What he doesn't realize is that you can't force a person to be with you, regardless of how much you love them. When you're done, you're just done. You can't force things that aren't meant to be. No matter how bad you may want something, holding on may be detrimental to your growth as a person. I'm at the point where I would rather choke on the truth than to suffocate while living a lie. I'm tired of living that lie with Aaron. We were with each other out of convenience and being comfortable in the only love—or lack thereof—we've ever known. I'm tired of it. I lost my zest for life long before I ever reached what was considered prime. Hell, I watered down myself to be his everything, while he lived his life fully. Thinking about that now has me pissed that I wasted good vagina years to nurture him and his bullshit. I was searching for something in him that I have yet to find.

I drop my keys on my kitchen counter as I contemplate

my next course of action. Aaron is a cancer, and in order to get rid of it, I need to find the nucleus and uproot it. I have to take drastic measures and take back control of my life. Starting after graduation, I'm done with this. Being that I am only three shy months away from graduation, I can handle the rest of this semester like a champ. I just need to focus. That and the added distraction of Kwame. He's a much-needed change in direction. Sure, I need to take time to heal, but a side of me knows I need to nurture what Kwame and I are going to grow. As if he can read my thoughts, a text comes through.

Kwame: *Thinking of you gorgeous, prayerfully you are having a great day. I'll be off grid for a little bit with all of the training I'm undergoing. One-month Gypsy ONE and then I'm coming for everything that is mine!*

I smile as I respond back. *Good luck on Combine and training babe. Everything that is yours will be waiting for your return. Just keep everything that is mine ALL mine and I'm firm on that (kissy face emoji)*

Kwame: *No doubt Gypsy, you just hold me down like the queen you are and we will be super straight. You're*

mine and I am yours. Handle business babe. I'm getting
ready for take-off talk to you soon (kissy face emoji)

I place my phone back down, knowing I need to purge these feelings and begin to write. The pen starts to flow, and as it flows, I notice through my anger, I'm penning my final goodbye to Aaron.

I hope she loves you
I pray she caters to your hopes
I long for her to magnify your dreams
I need the woman in her to speak to the man in you
Let her into your heart
Allow her to penetrate your soul
Taking you to a place I never could go
The potential I saw in you it is my desire that she digs up
and nurtures it
Let her speak life into your world
I pray YOU are ready to receive what she has to offer
I generally hope you are no longer a taker but a giver as
well
You see, my love, you can't constantly take from a
treasure and not check to see if the gold you once found is

getting low

I long for you to find that there is more to life than just a

pretty face and a wet yoni

Can't you shake the thoughts of wanting to be deep within

someone's sea enough to want to explore and captivate

one's soul?

Kinda like what we shared for a moment in time

You had me hooked up on a feeling

Sinking on a soul tie of sorts

I want you and your love to stop haunting my dreams

I need for us to truly let go

Why should I battle with you in my dreams as well as my

front door

I need for us to truly grow.

I long for us both to know there is a beauty in love

Safety in trust

Passion in giving

Hold up wait,

Wait a minute

You got me all in my feelings

But let's roll with this shit

I hope you love her

I pray you don't give up

I need for you to give her everything you couldn't give me

I long for you to never give up

It's one too many broken hearts in this world to add

another to the list

Give her attention and love baby just be her drug

Be her strength

Lead her into her destiny

Take it from me that scandalous unrequited love that shit

burns

Why do I even care

Seems as if by releasing you to her will get me out of my

feelings

Cured of you

Free to feel

No longer numb

I ultimately hope we let Go

I don't realize I'm crying until I drop the pen on my journal. Yes, it has only been a day of us truly being done, but I feel better. I feel light. I feel at peace. But it can be solidified in the fact that I'm done with everything Aaron a long time ago. My loyalty is what was keeping me in place. Actually, to be frank, it was holding me hostage—a bondage I desperately needed to break free of. I didn't want to start over. There was a sense of familiarity, so rather than break free, I chose to break my own heart and stay with a man that didn't appreciate me. But no longer will I be that girl. I thought no man could ever want me, but Kwame came along and changed that. I didn't think it was possible for me to feel again, but here I am, feeling and hoping. I know it will be a long journey ahead, but I'm willing to try. Hopefully, he is too.

Needing to shake the heaviness of my feelings and Aaron popping up at my door, I turn toward my Yamaha Clavinova Electric Piano and allow my fingers to flow over the keys until it eventually turns into a song. The melody soothes me, and eventually, I am belting out the lyrics to a song, giving it everything I have.

But there's a side to you
That I never knew, never knew
All the things you'd say

They were never true, never true

And the games you play

You would always win, always win

But I set fire to the rain

Watched it pour as I touched your face

Well, it burned while I cried

'Cause I heard it screaming out your name

Your name

Kwame

Leaving Gaea this morning had to be the hardest thing I've ever had to do. Not because I have fallen in love with her after she gave me a little taste of her pussy, but because it's all surreal and so very new to me. I want to capitalize on that moment and expand her thinking. I don't want to just be her rebound after her breakup. I also don't want her to jump feet first into what I'm trying to build with her. I need her to handle her business and her feelings with Aaron before making the conscious decision to be with me.

I'm all about healing her heart, but she has to want that too. Too often, people are walking into something brand new with the baggage of yesteryear. Honestly, they're doing themselves a disservice to hold on to what hurt them, while the other person is living footloose and fancy free. Why hold yourself hostage? If you've done everything you can to show a person how much you care and have given them love freely, and they still abuse it, then it's solely their loss. Fuck them. You shouldn't have to go around proving your love to anyone. What's the point? That's one of the sole reasons I only pour my feelings into my mother and sister. Well, and now the possibility of Gaea. But for now, I can't dwell on any of that. I have to focus. Football, family, and then love.

Talk about being lucky. Out of about 330 players, I was invited to come out and stand amongst the rest of the college greats and, well, ain'ts. The NFL combine in itself is a weeklong interview that will ultimately determine my draft status, salary, and ultimately, my entire career. Throughout this week-long interview, I'll take part in the forty-yard dash, Bench press, vertical jump, broad jump, twenty-yard shuttle, three-cone drill, sixty-yard shuttle, my own position-specific drills, interviews, physical measurements, injury evaluation, drug screen, the Cybex test, and the Wonderlic test. Even with going through all of that, I'm still super excited. Not only am I considered one of the greats entering the draft, but I'll be graduating from college. I'll be the first male in my family to do so. I'd be breaking the mold that was placed on me.

With graduation looming upon me, I'm thankful that this semester, I was able to take my last few classes online. I still have to go in and speak with my professors occasionally, but other than that, I'm able to train as freely as possible. My strengthening couch, Dre, is a beast, being a former NFL linebacker himself. He's been killing me to push me to the next level. I'm doing three-a-day drills with him, preparing to be amongst the greats. After drills, I condition my body to stay in tip-top shape. Most would say the position I played was challenging to play because it requires an error-free combination of both strength and speed. I'm trying to be amongst the greats like Von Miller and Ray Lewis.

The only thing holding me back from maximizing my potential is me. Well, not necessarily me, but more of the bane of my existence—Maxwell. He pops up at every training and conditioning session. He even shows up for my interview sessions that I have. When it comes time to form a team when I see that this is going to the next level, his ass is front and center with his shit-eating grin. He'd be around, and I'd ignore the hell out of him. It's petty, but rather than disrespect my father, I choose to ignore his ass and move on with my show. But the shit fucks with me and throws me off my game.

The more he shows up, the more I push harder to get away from him. He's the main reason I don't allow bullshit the opportunity to fester and make itself a home in my life. The shit is toxic, but I can't bring myself to disrespect him no matter how much I don't care for the man. I've watched my mother suffer because of him. From the beginning of my life, I can't remember him being in my life as consistently as he has been since football became a thing. I guess I'm his ticket out, but fuck all that. I'm not giving him shit!

I've watched my mother struggle to make shit happen, while he did whatever the fuck he wanted. He was so vile that when he would come by, he would have whatever woman he was involved with for that week sit in the car while he kicked the shit with us. I'm talking, this nigga would be playing home for hours sometimes. The sad part is he would fuck my mother during this time, give his dumbass advice, or rather opinions, of what I should be doing in regards to football, then he would leave like the shit was normal. It was obvious as hell that both my mother and the women knew about each other, being as my mother was very much pregnant with my sister.

I wanted so badly to be angry at my mother for allowing him to abuse her and her love in the way that he did. But how can I when she honestly didn't know any better? A woman that truly loves herself with the love of God would never let a man desecrate all over her life like he did. This is a woman who never missed a worship service, and she was allowing Satan all up and through her life. I admire her strength in other areas of her life, but this one here, I just pity her. I understand she's hurting because she didn't have a good representation of what love could be. Although we could clearly see she was hurting, she stayed and accepted any 'ol thing he threw her way because a little was better than nothing at all. She wanted a family, but all she gave me was a false narrative of family and a strong distaste in my mouth for a man that was, by birth and birth alone, my father.

This is why I need Gaea to heal. I can't stomach her going back and forth with me and my heart because she was confusing love with familiarity. Although I want her, I will have to cut her ass loose if I feel she isn't good for my heart. Damaged hearts can't do anything but damage yours. I'm not willing to take that bet for anyone. I can't. I have too much to lose and too many people counting on me to allow a heartbreak to slow me down and hold me stagnant.

"Kwam, get your fucking head in the game! We didn't come this far to go home with nothing! You owe me this shit for letting your mama keep you!" Maxwell spits out.

Nothing like seeing him show up to ruin my workout. I immediately stop pulling the tire that I'd been running with. I'm not in the mood for his shit. In fact, I again don't know who keeps telling his punk drunk ass when and where my trainings are. I have to get my head together if I want to be at least in the top ten. The top ten will ensure that I get my mother and sister away from him. I swallow the words that I know will have me on one of these gossip sites—hell, probably even ESPN. I don't have time for that shit. I need to protect my brand, so I push my earphones deeper into my ear and allow music to get me through this intense workout.

Naw, fuck all of you niggas; I ain't finished

Y'all don't wanna hear me say it's a goal
Y'all don't wanna see Wayne win fifty awards
I got real ones livin' past Kennedy Road
I got real ones with me everywhere that I go
I'm tryna tell ya, I got enemies, got a lotta enemies
Every time I see 'em, somethin' wrong with they memory
Tryna take the wave from a nigga
So tired of savin' all these niggas, mane!

I got enemies, got a lotta enemies
Got a lotta people tryna drain me of this energy
Tryna take the wave from a nigga
Fuckin' with the kid and pray for your nigga

"Great workout, kid. I'm proud of the progress you've made. The only thing I would suggest to you now is to find a way to put a muzzle on your old man. If you don't do it now, that shit is going to come back to bite yo' ass in the end. You think he's a monster now, and you're not making any money. Just think when you have millions at your disposal," Dre says with certainty.

"I hear you, Dre. But what can I possibly say? That's my dad. Despite him being not shit, and as much as I hate

82

to have his ass around, it's better for him to be where I can see him than to let him loose to terrorize my girls. Either way it goes, I am in a lose-lose situation, but in order to see them not fret a day, I'll deal with his antics," I say as I watch Maxwell go and schmooze some reporters who have been camped out in front of the gym I work out in. I'm sure that he's the one who leaked the information in order to create a buzz that wasn't needed. I now have people to create the buzz around me, and that isn't due to start until after the draft. But no, ever the eager Maxwell is tipping them, and it's probably to line his own pockets. But I can bet you your last wooden ass penny that he won't give a dime to my mother to take care of his daughter. No, he's much too good for that shit. I'm sure he will leave that shit for me to take care of.

"Hey, son!" he says, and I cringe, already anticipating the bullshit to come out of his mouth. "If you want to be amongst the greats, you must beat the greats. When Von Miller was in your position here at combine, he ranked second in the forty-yard dash, third in the vertical jump, first in the broad jump, third in the twenty-yard shuttle, first in the three-cone drill, and first in the sixty-yard shuttle. His 11.15-second sixty-yard shuttle broke the combine linebacker record. Not to mention that he ran a 4.49 forty-yard dash. So where is your head at in this game? Do you want to be great, or do you want to be the bitch your mother was trying to raise?"

"Just when I was about to give you the benefit of the doubt, you come in and say something about my mother. Be careful with your next words, Max, or you will live to regret it," I spit out in a whisper.

"Kwame, don't let this shit get to you. Don't make me have to knock you on your ass for even thinking of threatening me. I'm top dog, and you're just the nut yo' mammy wasn't smart enough to swallow," he says as he turns and leaves out of the gym.

If he were anybody else, I would've put his head through the God damn wall. But no. He's my father, and aren't I supposed to honor him even if he isn't so great to my family? Scripture says yes, so for now, I'm going to stick with that. One day, his day will come, and he will have to pay for his sins. I can't fuck this up now that I have a legit way to get us out the hood. But it won't be long until I'm no longer playing his bitch! Although I'm exhausted, I have to brush this shit off. I turn back toward the gym to find Dre cleaning up.

"Aye, what do you say we run another drill?" I ask as I lace up my kicks.

Draft Day

"With the second pick in the 2015 NFL draft, the Brownfield Bears select linebacker Kwame Jacobsen, from Brown State University."

I don't hear shit else after that. I immediately drop to my knees and pray. None of this would be possible had it not been for God showing his mercy for my family and me. I'm finally amongst the greats, finally living out my dream. I go up to collect my jersey and shake hands with the commissioner. After we are done celebrating, I meet with my team to formulate a plan and secure endorsements. Most players, I'm sure, are caught in the moment, but not me. No, I have a plan to execute so that I can get home to my baby. I would love nothing more than to be currently celebrating in the velvety cushion of her love canal. To have her caramel-colored breasts bouncing as I drill into her. To let her lust-filled moans float through the air like a soulful Sade song. Going with those thoughts and a raging hard on, I pick up the phone and dial her number, hoping to hear her voice drip sweetly through my ears like honey.

But I am not prepared for what I am greeted with. My heart drops into my feet.

We're sorry; we are unable to complete your call as dialed. Please check the number and dial again, or call your operator to help you.

What in the entire fuck? I guess she doesn't want to take a real chance at love with me after all. I could respect her more if she would have told me straight up that what I was offering had been too much for her. But no. I couldn't even get that. No lie, this shit feels like a gut punch. It's cool because from this point forward, I won't let anyone else get close enough to potentially break me down. Gaea and Maxwell are now in the same category. Not shit to Kwame!

Gaea

Three years later

You can do this, Gaea, I think to myself while I prepare for what can be one of my most personal performances. Performing is something I picked back up after I left Brown State. It's become my form of therapy. Using a gift to heal the heart is my moto. I'm ready for this. If only I can get out of my own head and get dressed. Had this been a couple years ago—hell, even a few short months ago—I would have blown this show out of the water. But that was before I decided to give into my grief. Hence my return to where it all started for me. The very thought of it now sends fire through my veins and a cold shiver down my spine.

"Pathetic!" I mumble as I continue to rummage through my closet for my lucky Giuseppe's. Maybe I shouldn't be as angry as I am at him; I should probably even thank him. Those three years of solitude did me some good. Things aren't perfect, but at least I am out of bed and not wallowing in my own sorrows. Who am I fooling? I still have my days where the shit is suffocating me. The difference between then and now is the fact that I have people watching and looking up to me now. I'm definitely in a much better space mentally and spiritually. Emotionally—well, that is improving.

"Gaea, did you say something?"

Shit. I forgot Anais was even here.

"Butterfly!"

"Oh, I'm sorry, Ana. I didn't hear you."

"Lies. Look, Gaea, you have nothing to be worried about; you are about to bring down the house in Amour Noir tonight! I'm surprised you're even…"

Little does she know, that is the farthest thing from my mind. I'm confident in my skill sets; what's eating me now is the possibility of running into anyone I've been trying to avoid for the last couple of years. If anyone I know from my past happens to be there tonight, I need to look damn good to prove to at least myself that I am absolutely OK and that I broke the spell of his charm.

"Yeah. How has the dance studio been?" I quickly change the subject. I am not going down *that* road tonight. That would be all I need to lose the courage and jump right back into bed. I love her, but she has this weird way of making me talk about things that I would rather keep buried.

"Oh, same ol', same ol', holding auditions, sewing costumes, giving a lot of TLC. Why? Are you ready to join the team?"

"That would definitely be a no. I can't leave the trauma world behind. They need me." I giggle. Ana knows I take my nursing career seriously. I can't fathom giving that up to chase around a bunch of toddlers—or adults who act like toddlers. "But I can swing by to get a couple of eight counts in with you."

"You should. It'll make up for the time you've missed out on while you were gone."

I know my leaving hurt her, but it was something I needed to do to become a better me. Not only for me, but for the people that are looking up to me. I needed to purge and re-center to focus on what had become distant.

"I'm sorry, Ana."

"No need for an apology. I'm just happy to have my sister back and overly ecstatic to see you sing again. But you better have your ass in the studio after you complete your first week at the hospital."

"Good, now help me find an eccentrically sexy ensemble that will help me set this club stage on fire."

I stuff the rest of my nerves in a box and begin to rummage through my closet for the perfect outfit. We settle on a nude Krista sequined fringe dress by Herve Leger, my nude Harmony Sparkle Giuseppe's, and beautiful accents from Tiffany's glistening my ears, wrist, and neck.

Perfect.

Now, all I have left to do is give myself a lightweight, natural beat and take down my twist-out, and my look will be complete.

"See you tonight, belle. Sing us a good ol' nasty ballad that'll for sure get me close enough to slap the black off of Tobias's ass."

"Sure thing, sis!" I say as I close my front door, giggling, reminding myself that some things never change. I'm sure she isn't trying to, but she makes me even more nervous.

*****

"Let's all give Torque a round of applause! Amour

Noir appreciates your craft!" a coffee-colored, robust man announces. "Now, coming to the stage is a Goddess that has been missing from the scene for quite some time. It's safe to say, due to the packed house, that her presence has been missed. Please join me in giving a warm welcome back to not only someone near and dear to my heart and the songstress to my soul—"

"Alright now, Anthony! Don't get slapped up there!" a caramel-brown honey yells with a smile, and the crowd erupts with laughter

"Y'all forgive my lovely wife, Brielle, there." He laughed but then continued. "Someone that is near and dear to *our* hearts and the songstress to our souls. Our sister from another mister and the very reason we are together today—Ms. Gaea Lee!"

The crowd gives a loud welcome. I hold up a hand and wait for the crowd's applause to die down before I speak.

"Thanks for the introduction, Ant. It means a lot coming from you and Bri!" I say and wink before I address the audience. "Hello, Amour Noir. It is my pleasure to be back in the comfort of what I consider to be my safe haven.

I have missed you all intensely. Tonight, I am going to sing from my heart in hopes you all understand my spirit a little more." I place a hand over my heart and take a deep breath as the piano begins to play this lugubrious tune. I begin to sing my very own rendition of Jill Scott's *Hear My Call.*

"Here I am again, asking questions…"

I begin to command the stage, making it my very own. With every word, I feel as though I am giving the audience a little peep into my soul, and suddenly, I am OK with the world seeing my pain.

"God, please hear my call…"

"Love has burned me raw…"

In this song, I feel all of the weight, all of the tears, and all of the emotions I've been forced to deal with on my own. With fluid conviction, I push through this song as if I'm depending on it for my next breath. I pour new determination into this song to push past my past and guarantee more sunshine. I'm tired of the dark cloud keeping me from being happy. My hunger is no longer derived from the need of attention but from the need to be with my true authentic self.

"Love has turned me cold. I need your healing. Please. Please. Please..."

There isn't a dry eye in the house as I end the song. The crowd erupts, giving me a standing ovation, and I stand there with a look of shock, raw with emotion. I take my bow, and just like that, I leave the stage.

"That was exhilarating, and although it has made me feel a bit vulnerable, I can't help but to feel free. I mean, I have finally let go of all of the hurt and the pain that has held me back for years."

My friend Jennifer smiles and says, "Gaea, I am just happy to have you back. I know you are coming off of your stage high, but I must say this one thing. The best thing you could have ever done was to rid yourself of the baggage of your past. You are a beautiful, educated woman with a generous heart, who is worthy of being loved the right way."

"As much as it pains me to say it, Jenn is right, Butterfly," Anais adds in while fixing her headful of curls. Tonight, she's a force to be reckoned, and she's working the hell out of those Gucci Duchesse green, wide-leg, cuffed pants, paired with a black A.L.C. Cheyenne off-the-shoulder top and the black Scalopump by none other than Christian Louboutin himself. "The three of us look too good tonight to let the likes of Aaron's trifling ass mess up our reunion. Fuck him." Little does she know, it's not only Aaron that has caused me pain.

"I hear you both! I love you ladies."

"Keep that emotional ass I love you reserved for girls' night. I'm ready to fuck up the dance floor," Ana adds while grooving to whatever is playing.

Jennifer hugs me and then says, "Ana! That mouth! Ugh! Now, belle, let's go out on the dance floor and celebrate you coming back home so we can triple our blessings." Ana rolls her eyes under her thick lashes, and I chuckle as we head to the dance floor.

I have to admit that it feels great to be back and in the comfort of my friends and family. We make our way to the floor, and they are playing one of my favorite throwbacks but not that far back— "Yoga" by Janelle Monae and Jidenna. I instantly close my eyes and start my slow wind, getting lost in the music.

Truth be told, I wasn't really enjoying myself while away. All that I seem to have gotten from that trip besides clothing and shoes is a fatter ass and a clear understanding that Aaron was never my soulmate and that I shouldn't trust just anybody with my heart no matter how convincing the pillow talk is. If I'm being completely honest with myself, Aaron wasn't anything but a glorified sex buddy with the right credentials on my checklist of what it takes to be my husband. Ha! That list caused me nothing but trouble.

As the song begins to end, I make my way off the dance floor, informing Jennifer and Anais I'm going to the bar. Nothing like liquid courage to keep the night going and to keep me smiling. As I am making my way through the crowd, I am stopped by a few club goers to congratulate me on my performance tonight. Many are questioning when I will perform again, and I honestly haven't given it much thought. My main focus is to get this performance out of the way, dive deep into work, and actually heal. Who has time for being sad and heartbroken when you have shit to do and shit to accomplish?

"Butterfly?"

Shit! Not tonight. This could not be happening!

"If you are gonna capitalize off of our diminutive hiatus, the least you could've done was answer a text or a phone call."

I roll my eyes and hiss, "Fuck off, Aaron!"

"Oh, that mouth. I've missed you too, babe." Aaron chuckles,

"Save the bullshit! What do you want?"

"Just one quick thing, love, and don't cause a scene!"

"Cause a scene? Were you thinking about a God damn scene when you—" I caught myself. There was no way in hell I was about to let him reduce me to tears in this damn club. "You know what, Aaron! You can have whatever it is you think you need to say. I'm not interested. Now get the hell away from me."

"Listen here. You can be mad, but what I won't allow you to do is disrespect me…"

"You have two seconds to walk away from me."

"Babe, our table is ready… Oh, I'm sorry to interrupt," a honey-colored bombshell says. "What a beautiful performance; it was so heartfelt. The bastard that hurt you is a fool. You're gorgeous. I'm Kehli." She holds her hand out for a handshake.

"Nice to finally meet you face to face, Kehli. Thank you for your kind words," I say with my nice-nasty smile. "Aaron, it was dreadful seeing you again. Enjoy the rest of your night."

"Aaron? Wait you two know each other? Aaron! Answer me! Gaea? I've only followed all of your videos since forever, but you went off grid about six months ago." It's as if she suddenly recognizes who I am when she blurts out, "I'm so, so sorry. I didn't know. It's not what you think. I came along after you two were done. I promise."

"Kehli, will you just shut up? Go secure our table; I'll be right over."

"But—"

"Go now!" Aaron roars, bringing attention to where we're standing. Kehli darts off as if she can't believe what has just transpired.

"Butterfly, before you say another word, hear me out."

"You honestly think I want to hear *anything* you would

like to say to me? The nerve of you… You bring her here, of *all* places! *Here*? My God!" I say in a huff, mad at myself for even giving a damn about him and the ghost of bimbos' past. But as I turn to walk off, he grabs my arm.

"You will not continue to disrespect me. You wanted space. I gave you just that, but this behavior will not be tolerated," he says as he tightens his grip.

"No. What will not be tolerated is you putting your hands on me as if I owe you anything. The best thing you can do for the both of us is to let my arm the fuck go and walk away before whatever you *think* this is grows."

"You little bit—"

"You better be careful with the next works that come out of your mouth, you spineless bitch! Now let me the fuck go!" I say, snatching my arm from him.

"Tell me it isn't true that you left town to have and raise my baby!"

I glance up to see if anyone is watching us or even still paying attention, and to my unfortunate surprise, I see a stunned Tobias. Although it is clear his nosy ass heard, he's only trying not to give any indication that at the mention of the word 'baby,' he's as stunned as anyone else who knew me back then. I went away, but it's not as though I purposely hid my baby. I had my reasons to disappear, but none of those reasons involved hiding my daughter from Aaron. He was the furthest thing from my frightened little mind.

"I did no such thing!"

"You lying bitch! My daughters are in the same preschool! Only one of them knows me, and you're to blame for that."

"I'm sorry to break it to you, jackass, but my daughter doesn't belong to you," I say with finality.

I am well aware of who her father is and who it isn't. I've gone through great lengths to be sure. Her father is a man I once respected and thought the world of. But as with all things in my past, that was all a façade to get a piece of the healing heart I call me. It's always the broken ones that enter my world and take all the pieces they need to make themselves whole, only to leave me dispirited and struggling to hold it together at the end. So no, he isn't her father, and neither is the man I conceived her with.

Kynsley is mine, and I'm damn tired of hiding the fact that she's here.

"Then who does she belong to? The only other male you hung out with was... You scandalous bitch..."

"You have one more time to disrespect her, and I will put your head through that wall, Aaron," a visibly upset Tobias says. "It's obvious you two need to talk. But it will not happen here, nor will it be tonight. Walk away, man."

In this moment, I am happy to see Tobias is still his nosy, protective self. But from the look in his eyes, I can tell I'm far from off the hook. But before I can open my mouth to explain, I hear the DJ say, *"Club Amour Noir, look who just entered the building! Please join me in giving Kwame "Flash X" Jacobsen a warm welcome!"* I instantly feel warm all over, and everything is black. This cannot be life.

Kwame

I can't shake the events of the club appearance I did a few days ago; the proof of that was evident in the sloppy foot drills and the missed catches I bullshitted my way through. What are the odds that the siren that has caused me to lose sleep for the last three years was finally in the same place as me? I have so much I need to say to her, but I knew with the amount of anger I had in me, I couldn't bring myself to approach her. That and the fact that I saw her and Aaron engaged in a heated conversation.

"Kwam, get your head out of yo' ass boy! Move them feet! It's a lot of hungry men out there, vying to get their chance at your spot!"

What the fuck was he doing here? I think, but I know better than to voice it with all of those people around. It seems the more coverage I get, the more games I win, and the more endorsements I receive. Maxwell T. Jacobsen, my father, is forcing his way into my life. I tried unsuccessfully to rid myself of him by staying quiet and not engaging with him unless absolutely necessary, but just like cancer, when you ignore it, he stuck and spread himself all over my life. I couldn't pay the man to be a part of my life when we were struggling in the hood, but now he's here front and center. I shake those thoughts and place my focus on where it's needed: my job. I'll deal with his overbearing ass later.

Throughout practice, I'm bombarded with thoughts of Gaea. I can't, for the life of me, understand why she walked away from me and everything that I offered her. I gave her a month to clear things up so that she would be available to me so that I could restore all that was broken inside of her. But no, she took that month, and she disappeared. That shit gutted me. I thought for sure that my friend would nurture my heart and know the severity of what that one night meant to me, but no. Like the evil siren she is, she defecated all over my desires. I was left with two choices: let that heartbreak drown me, or let it be another driving force to help me succeed.

"There you go, Flash. Glad to see you check back in."

I give a backward nod at my coach and push through the rest of practice with precision. I have already made up my mind that before the end of today, I'm going to get my answers from Gaea whether she likes it or not.

After practice, I head over to Central Sports to get this interview out of the way. I dread going to these things because as of late, it's no longer just questions about the game. It's about where I stand socially, never morally, with the kneeling for the national anthem. That's when my biggest dilemma forms. I don't know whether to straddle the line and pussyfoot around it or go straight for the jugular and give them the unadulterated Colin Kaepernick mixed with a lot of Muhammad Ali version. The later version won out.

I spent the last half hour of my life explaining how I love and respect our troops. How although I didn't enlist, I understand the sacrifice they gave in the name of our country. But none of that can make me believe that a flag was worthier of respect than the life of an American person who just so happened to be African American. That the flag was not more important than policies that led to longer sentencing, the disparities in the legal system and laws in general, and the blood that was shed as a result of police officers. No. No one will change my opinions otherwise.

When told I wasn't one in the position to feel as if I were oppressed because, after all, I'm a millionaire, I felt I had to act in accordance with my thoughts and reply.

"By all means, let me be frank, and I need you to quote me verbatim. Although my financial wealth has changed, I am by all means an African American male in America. I am three times as likely to be pulled over in my own neighborhood for looking suspect. I am still the same Kwame Langston Jacobsen that grew up in the hood and was subjected to the harassment of being stopped because I fit the description of a suspect.

"I am also the same man that knows if it wasn't for my status as an NFL player, then I would still be pulling to move myself out the hood. My wealth may change, my popularity will change, but you know what won't? My blackness. I could be pulled over today despite my status in the NFL; the police don't care about that. The only thing they saw was my big black ass in a fancy car. Here I am, saying my people are oppressed, and you're telling me I can't relate to that struggle, because of a status change. Think again. Those that are not oppressed cannot pick and choose who they deem oppressed. Our struggles may be different, but in all means of the word, I am right there with them."

I go on to further explain that if they are so worried about the troops, then they need to meet me at the local VA to give the troops what they really need.

"We talk about the troops in theory and about respecting them. What exactly are the people of America doing to help them? We are using their act of sacrifice and service to push an agenda that doesn't align with the cause they are rallying against. You want to talk about respecting veterans? Let's start by reaching them where they are needing help. Do we realize when they come home, they are not getting access to adequate healthcare, mental healthcare, and the basic need of respect to the great sacrifice they've given? I know firsthand because I am there, volunteering my time, my heart, and my money. Because contrary to popular belief, I can stand down in the trenches with both spectrums."

After taking some time to go over my stats and what to expect in this upcoming season, we bring the interview to a close. No sooner than I make it to my car, I see missed calls—one from my sister and at least twenty from my mother. I call Kalyse, but I get no answer, so I call my mother.

"Hey, gorgeous. What's going on?"

"Kwame, it's Kalyse. Get here as fast as you can."

"Where are you?"

"Memorial Baptist Hospital."

My heart drops. "I'm on my way."

*****

After getting to the hospital, checking in with my mother, and thoroughly ignoring my father, I take a minute to pray. There is no one to bring me peace like God. I just can't believe my fifteen-year-old sister is fighting for her life. She was stabbed and left to die by someone she called her best friend—all over some shoes and a little boy neither of the two girls should've been involved with in the first place. I can't lose her; that's my baby. As I am asking God to grant me mercy and to show me a sign that everything will be OK, I hear a voice as sweet as honey and as smooth as silk.

"Kwame, is that you?" *Oh, God, you have a twisted form of humor.* The very woman I was going to seek out is now at my feet, but I know now is not the time to address my grievances with her.

"In the flesh," I say trying, unsuccessfully to hide the disgust I felt in my voice.

"I thought that was you," she says as she shifts her feet. "Well, for the sake of formalities, I'm Gaea, and I will be the nurse in charge of your sister's care. If you would be so kind as to follow me, Dr. Milo would like to have a word with you and your family."

Did this muthafucka just use her professional voice on me? Like we don't fucking know each other? It's taking everything in me to not curse her ass out in this hospital. But I am not trying to end up on TMZ for the amount of unchecked emotions I'm about to spit out. Three God damn years, and all I get is a generic ass, "I thought that was you." She must have forgotten who the fuck I am. But before I can check her ass on the slick, Tobias walks up, looking back and forth at us, trying to figure out what she's doing here. She then motions toward her badge with an attitude, putting her hands on her voluptuous hips with a huff.

"Hey, Gaea, can you make sure that this floor is secure and that no one is able to access Kalyse? There are a shitload of reporters outside."

"Did you just… I know you…" She clears her throat and puts on that plastic ass professional voice again. "Tobias, I will inform the hospital of this issue."

With that out of the way, I drag my heavy feet to my sister's room where my mother and Maxwell are already there and waiting for me to join. As I enter the room, Dr. Milo begins to tell us that they finally have Kalyse stable, but for right now, they had to put her into a medically-induced coma due to the amount of trauma she's sustained. He goes on to tell us that God must have really been on her side because out of the thirty-six times she was stabbed, only one nicked an artery. We're informed that we need to be prepared for an uphill battle of recovery.

After hearing this all and taking the majority of it in, I can't hold all the anger I feel inside in. I start to bawl. I just can't imagine the amount of pain baby girl is going through. She looks so angelic, lying in that bed, but still so lifeless. It's beginning to be too much for me, and to make matters worse, Maxwell is attempting to comfort me.

"We will get through this together, son."

"Max, can you just not? I don't need this right now. Just give me my space!" I growl out. How dare he come along now, in our time of need, pretending to be this doting father when we all know he is just an opportunist. I look over at my beautifully demure and meek mother and hold my mule. I know now in this moment, I need to go get a cup of Jesus and an extra shot of Jerusalem to not lose every bit of sanity and religion I have left in me. I walk over to my mother and kiss her cheek, letting her know I will be in the lobby if she needs me.

What they don't know is that baby girl is my strength. She's the sun in my otherwise cloudy world. My success is for her. I knew when I moved them out of the hood, I should've changed everything else around her too, including the school she was at. I could've done more to protect her.

As I enter the lobby, I look around in hopes that I can spot Tobias in the lobby. He seems to always know the right words to keep me centered. But to my surprise, I see him engaged in what seems to be a heated conversation with Gaea about what I am assuming is about the safety of baby girl. I head over to dead the conversation, but nothing prepares be for what I walk up on.

"About your daughter." *Her daughter.* "Is she Kwame's?" I hear Tobias inquire.

"The short answer to that is yes."

"Are you positive?"

I have a daughter?

"How dare you ask me some simple shit like that? Yes, Kynsley is 99.9 percent his. Now if you would excuse me, I'd like to return back to work. I've had enough of being disrespected today."

"Gaea, talk to him. You need to tell him if he doesn't know."

Before she can continue on with her charade, I charge at them like a bull to a matador. Not only did she disappear years ago, but apparently, she was pregnant.

"How dare you! How old is she?" I spit, unable to control my anger.

"Kwame, you have your nerve! My daughter is two and a half, not that you care."

Not that I care? What the fuck is she talking about?

"Kwam, calm down. You will get your answers," Tobias says while cutting a look at Gaea. "But right now, in this moment, your sister needs you."

I pull my emotions back in and collect myself. Kalyse needs me. I'm going to use everything in my power to see to it that she's OK, but this shit here gutted me. Not only could I have lost my sister today due to a coward, but I'm also faced with a very real fact that a woman I thought the world of has been keeping a baby from me.

"I can't deal with this shit right now. Un-fucking-believable! Let me go handle things with my mother, but you haven't heard the last from me."

Gaea

Yesterday had been a blur for me, starting with Kynsley. Some days, I can't even remember how I managed to have a full-blown career and handle her all the same with little to no help at all. Ana and my parents are a Godsend, but I don't always have them. Kynsley has been hell on wheels from the moment her feet hit the floor, and by the time we make it to Ana's studio, she's somewhat back to normal. I guess the move here is affecting her more than I thought.

By the time I made it to work and got a report from the nurse on the previous shift, I had Kynsley and her adjustment processed heavily on the brain. But all seemed to stand still the moment a teenage version of my daughter was rushed into the hospital. It completely winded me for a second before I hightailed it into gear. In those intense moments, it never struck me that maybe, just maybe, this beautiful, angelic face was none other than Kwame's sister and my daughter's aunt. The most surreal part was that once she was out of surgery, she was assigned to my floor, and her case was assigned to me.

Once I saw Kwame in the waiting room, I had to collect my thoughts and adjust my attitude so that I could do my job as best I could without letting my anger spill out on him. In those few seconds, I took in the beauty that was him. There he was, standing at an even six feet four, rich, mocha skin, almond-shaped eyes a warm abyss of brown, with a muscular, athletic build with beautifully bowed legs. The only noticeable difference I could see was his curly hair was longer, and his beard was thicker. He looked so good that I wanted to straddle his face. Then I remembered I hated his arrogant, inconsiderate ass. What totally blew my mind was the way he looked at me as I approached him as if I were the who had wronged him. We get past the awkwardness that is us, and Tobias's ass chooses that day of all days to corner me with questions of Kynsley's paternity. Like I didn't have to go through paternity prior to today. But what shocked me is that Kwame acted like he didn't know. The shit blew me.

As I watch my baby glide and slide all over the floor, I can't help but think of how someone couldn't want to be a part of such greatness. But of course, I would think that about my baby. I'm OK with being biased.

"Butterfly, do you think there is some truth to Kwame not knowing? If we are being completely honest here, you never actually talked to him, right?"

"Ana, he had almost two and a half years to make things right. It doesn't matter how he found out; the fact of the matter is that it got to him. What is very clear is that he knew. I mean, come on. If his camp knew, I'm sure he knew; otherwise, how and why else would he be sending money in the form of a cashier's check every month?"

"Don't be so sure, Butterfly," Ana says as she takes a sip of coffee and proceeds to correct some of Kynsley's dance steps. "Bumblebee, you have to move your feet like this."

As they continue working out the kinks to their choreography, I step away to make a cup of my Blueberry Bliss tea to shake the thoughts of Kwame. But the efforts are in vain. My thoughts drift into the fact that maybe there is a slim possibility that he wasn't aware. But how could that even be possible? Even with the minute possibility that somehow, we snuck through the cracks, it still didn't begin to explain why he never reached out. He had been so adamant that he was taking on the challenge to heal my heart. Only when I opened my heart to the possibility of it, he fumbled it and let it fall through the cracks. What stung the most is that unlike Aaron, he never made the effort to come after me. To come after us.

So in theory, I wasn't as important as I was made to believe. No, I was foolish yet again when it came to my heart, and that made me feel so low. But not low enough that it stunted my need to be a mother. But that didn't mean I wasn't angry; I was angrier than a muthafucka. Angry because despite his not being in our daughter's life, he let me down. He led me to believe that he could love me. But it turns out instead of being the friend that I needed him to be, he played on my vulnerable state things fast, and left me broken. Kwame was just like any other man, thinking with his dick. He gave me all that bullshit about taking care of my heart, but he left in an even uglier state than it was prior to me opening myself up to him.

116

He took advantage of the opportunity to have my heart and traded it for a chance at having my pussy. That shit hurt and crippled my already fragile heart. No matter how often I try to purge these thoughts, I hold it close to the point it nearly suffocates me. I hold it because my hurt has nowhere else to go but in.

When my second batch of tea is done brewing, I peek in on my sister and daughter to make sure they are doing OK. Hearing my baby giggle and seeing that they are seemingly fine, I know that I am OK with sneaking away for a while. Upon entering my bedroom, I see, laying on top of some of Kynsley's drawings, one of my favorite poems by Iyanla Vanzant titled *Yesterday I Cried*. I read over it a few times before I start my meditation practice. After the week I've had, I need to align my chakras so that I'm not transferring negative energy to my daughter.

After about an hour, I am feeling lighter and like a positive beam of light. I join my sister and daughter for some much-needed girl bonding. We spend our afternoon playing a couple of rounds of Just Dance and The Michael Jackson experience, watching Kynsley's favorite movie, "The Princess and the Frog," for the millionth time, and beginning to prepare dinner after the kid is laid out for a late nap.

"Gaea, can I offer some unsolicited advice?" Ana asks, knowing even if I say no, she'll continue on anyway.

"Umm, sure. Go for it," I say as I prepare the chicken and andouille sausage for the alfredo we are having for dinner.

"Butterfly, I can see your pain no matter how you try to mask it. My heart hurts for you because underneath all the beauty that is you, I see a broken, frightened little girl," Ana states as she locates the asparagus in the fridge. "It's OK to hurt, and it's certainly OK to feel sad. Those are your feelings, and they are valid. But what is not OK is to allow that hurt to sink in and change who you are at the core."

"But I haven't changed, Ana. Other than becoming a mother to Kynsley," I state matter-of-factly.

"Gaea, but you have, darling. Your heart is cold. When was the last time you've done something for you? When was the last time you've been out with a guy?"

"I don't have time for things like that. Besides, I don't need a guy to pillow talk me and get—"

"My point exactly! You've allowed a few guys who weren't worthy rob you and help you to bury what is innate, Butterfly," she says as she pulls me into her arms. "Stop holding onto the pain of boyfriends' past. Think of 2 Timothy 1:7—*For God did not give us the spirit of timidity, but a spirit of power, of love, and of self-discipline.* Let go, baby. Know that you are never alone in this journey; I'm standing with you ten toes down. Not only that, but God has you."

When she speaks those words, it's like a dam has broken. I crumble; everything that I held within my soul pours out. And just as the poem said, I'm crying, and this time, it's with an agenda.

Kwame

I can't, for the life of me, fathom why Gaea would keep the possibility of my being someone's father away from me. That shit was mind boggling. On top if that, I am in the middle of a media shit storm due to my interview and President Orange calling for my job. The only solace is that after the news broke of Kalyse, they gave me some reprieve. Now those things, I can deal with and handle like it's nothing. But this shit with Gaea— nope, nah, hell no, that shit isn't shaking. It's my hope to run into her during my visits with my sister, but it seems she conveniently goes on lunch break or just not be around during the ICU visiting hours, which explains why I am sitting in front of her house now.

Thank God for Anais coming through with an address when I ran into her at the grocery store. Hell, as is, I'm not going to be able to rest until I get the answers that I need. For three years, she's been holding this secret from me. Three years. I could've possibly missed out on my child's life. I need her to tell me she didn't purposely do this. I swallow the bitterness and anger I feel as I exit my satin, black model S Tesla. I make my way to the front door of a small Spanish-style home with a beautifully manicured lawn. The sunflowers planted out front give me the biggest clue I need to know I was at the right house. I take a timid breath and mumble a prayer before I knock on the door.

Reveal Your wise ways, God. Give me a pure heart, and may my words reflect Your truth as I enter into this space of uncertainty.

"Ana! I don't know how many times I've had to… Oh!" Gaea says as she tightens her grip around the towel that is wrapped around her. "I wasn't expecting anyone— or you for that matter. But I can't say this visit isn't needed. Come on in, and make yourself comfortable. Give me a moment to change, and I'll be right back out."

She leads me into a rustic farmhouse-styled kitchen before disappearing into the back of the house. I take a moment to take in my surroundings. Unlike spunky attitude from the years prior, everything in her space gives off a more modest feel with lots of sprinkles of her daughter. I can tell from the artwork-covered refrigerator

121

that her daughter is the center of her universe. The artwork is, what I assume, a chocolate ballerina with larger-than-life hair and a few Mommy and me pictures. I look a little further, and there's one that really captures my eye and makes me feel things that are unfamiliar for me to be feeling for a little person I'd never even met. Hell, I still have no clue what she looks like. But low and behold, this picture of the same little girl with larger-than-life hair and what I assume is supposed to be her dad. Albeit stick figures with an abundance of color, I'm immediately pissed the fuck off. *Who is this nigga?* I think as I run my hands across the picture, letting out a deep groan.

"Wishful thinking on her part; the kid has a very active imagination," she says as a form of an explanation, letting off a nervous giggle. "Would you like something to drink? Tea? Blueberry, of course. Water? Hennessey?"

I choke back a laugh, seeing as I'm still fuming, and she's trying to make light of the situation. I take a moment to take her in, and she's still gorgeous. The only significant differences I can see are that her breasts are fuller, her hips a bit curvier, and her wet curls are longer. But her bare face is what's holding me. It's still stunning. I shake my head to get out of the trance she has me in.

"Nah, Gyp—Gaea. I'm good."

"OK, well, let's get to it. To what do I owe the pleasure of this visit?"

"What we are not gonna do is skirt around this baby's—"

"Kynsley. Her name is Kynsley."

"Right. Kynsley… Let's not pussyfoot around the issue of her."

"What would you like to know, Kwame?" she asks with a hint of annoyance that she quickly masks.

"Start at the beginning, and don't leave anything out."

She shifts uncomfortably, clears her throat, and says, "The beginning." She starts worrying with her lip, and for a second, she looks scared. But as quickly as I see the fear and uncertainty, in an instant, it's gone. I don't know what to make of that, so I gather my bearings and wait for her to start. She clears her throat, and begins to tell me what she knows I need to know.

She goes on to explain that upon learning she was pregnant, she came looking for me and ways to get in contact with me because my month away turned out to be a full three months away. She states she had tried calling me multiple times, but because we had both changed our numbers, she couldn't reach me. She felt defeated after being unsuccessful in reaching me, so she went on with her pregnancy and, ultimately, her life.

She proceeds to tell me that Kynsley was born three months premature, but with the help of her parents and her sister, she was able to further her career, earning her Master's in nursing. Hearing that she had to make some sacrifices and that she had to face this alone starts to pick away at the anger that has settled in my heart. Just looking at her now, with her face encased in curls, I see strength and a whole lot of wisdom.

"What's her full name, Gaea?"

"Kynsley Zora-Leigh Jacobsen."

I choked on air, being completely stunned that she'd given her daughter my last name despite my not knowing about and her dropping her feelings for me either way into an abyss of darkness. To say I'm pissed off again would be an understatement. Who in the fuck does she think she is? How do you purposely give a child someone else's last name but fail to tell the father about the God damn child. I'm not that lame ass nigga Aaron she was fucking around with. I, for one, am not about to let her get away with this bullshit. I probably should've prayed harder because I want to call up my cousins to shake some sense into her silly ass.

"Why? How could you do this? Help me to under-fucking-stand!"

Seemingly unmoved by my anger, she takes a sip of her tea, places her teacup covered in music notes down, and glares at me. "First off, watch your tone, and lower your voice. Yelling isn't gonna solve a damn thing. So if you can check that shit real quick, I can answer you as best as I can."

I know this muthafucka didn't just try to check me, I think to myself as I calmed my nerves.

"Just answer the God damn question, Gaea. You knew how I felt first-hand about the ramifications of making someone a single mother. Knowingly or not, this shit is foul no matter how you paint the muthafucka to make it pretty. You knew my hardship coming up in a single-parent home and how I loathed anyone making babies and leaving them to be raised alone."

Sitting in complete silence, looking me over with a delicately arched eyebrow and those coffee-brown saucers she had for eyes causes me to shift uncomfortably. I'm waiting for her to explode, pleading for her to go toe to toe with me. I don't get how she doesn't understand this shit is truly fucking with me. Something flashes in her eyes, and again, she quickly shakes it off, clears her throat, and continues.

"When I knew I was pregnant, and I couldn't reach you, I left. I could not allow myself to stay stuck while carrying our child. It was bad enough I was in a toxic environment. Kyns wasn't Aaron's, so that was my out. I was dead wrong for not telling you, but I needed to get me together for her. If you want paternity established, then do that to ease your mind, but she is yours. Be angry at me, but don't you dare take your hate for me out on her. She's innocent. You both deserve each other—period," she spits out with firm finality.

"I won't meet her until I know…"

Before I can even finish, a tiny bundle of chocolate perfection with a mass of jet-black curls comes running through, and my heart clenches. There's no denying that she's mine. She bounces over to her mother, giving her a big smile. She's beautiful. She has my bountiful lashes, big, brown, baby doll eyes, and still a bit of baby fat. She's dressed in what seems to be dance gear with tiny tap shoes. My vision blurs. I can't believe that I'm actually someone's father, and the hurtful part of it all is that I missed out on her for two and a half years.

"Mommy, I misseded you so much! TT Ana was being a big meanie today." I heard her say.

"I missed you too, Sweet Pea! Come. Let's go get some juice, and we can talk about it more later."

"OK, but Momma, who is that? He looks sad."

"Oh, this is Mommy's…"

"Hi, Kynsley, I'm your dad."

I hear Gaea take in a sharp breath and drop the mug she was holding.

"My dad? You mean I really have a dad? I prayed for one."

Gaea

"My dad? You mean I really have a dad? I prayed for one."

That sentence has been playing around in my head for a solid week. Not the fact that he revealed himself to be her father or the fact that she was OK with what he said being true. But it stems from the fact that although I thought I was giving Kynsley everything I thought she could ever need, she clearly knew she needed to go to God to bring her what her heart most desired. Yet here I am at the coffee shop, meeting with the man that deprived her of having a dad—her grandfather.

"Maxwell, to whom do I owe this pleasure?" I ask sarcastically.

"Cut the theatrics, girl. I told you to stay away. I've paid you handsomely, yet you're here!" he spits out.

"What we are not going to do is have you sit up in this coffee shop and disrespect me," I say as I lay out the spread of checks he'd been sending to keep me quiet and Kynsley hidden after I refused to get an abortion. There are some things you aren't allowed to tell a woman what to do with, and the decision to have my child was one of them. It was so easy for me to believe in my heart that Kwame sent his father to do his dirty work. But the look in Kwame's eyes the day he laid eyes on Kynsley let me know that he truly had no idea that he was someone's father, let alone Kynsley's.

"You're going to ruin his life. His future was set and having this—"

"This what? His daughter? No, she wasn't conceived under the best circumstances, but she's here. My beautiful, vivacious little girl is here, and regardless of what you try to say, she will remain in her father's life. Either you tell him what you did, or I will. As for those checks, you can keep them. I never had a need for them, nor does she!" I growl out as I place enough money on the table to cover my tea and a huge tip, leaving him and those damn checks on the table.

"You'll regret fucking with me, little girl."

"And you will regret underestimating me, old man," I say with a wink as I walk out the door.

I need the comfort of my sister, and stat. She can help me to make sense of all of this. Like how can this man be so vile to rob his son of this precious gift? I mean, if I really think about it, maybe he was trying to keep the dysfunctional shit he was spitting going. Only he hadn't met a mother like me. I do not play when it comes down to my child.

I pick up my phone and dial Ana.

"Butterfly, I'm in the middle of class. I'll meet you at Noir tonight before your performance. You are still doing it, right?"

"Shit, Ana! I forgot all about it. I have a lot to share."

"I know, I know… Kwame! Anyhow, I gotta jet. See you and Jenn later!"

The lunch—or lack thereof—with Maxwell left me feeling empty and, apparently, scatterbrained. I can't remember the last time I have forgotten something as important as performing. Good thing it is for the sole purpose of healing than it is a career. Because currently, my brain is full of figuring out this whole Maxwell situation. I can't possibly imagine my parents doing something so cruel. Well, my mother, Janet? Yeah, but my father, Theodore? Never! But being that he did, here I am, trying to make the transition as easy as possible for Kynsley. After meeting her father, that was all she could talk about. That, and the fact that for the last week and a half, Kwame was filling my house with a ridiculous amount of gifts. He's, without a doubt, overcompensating for the amount of time missed, and Kynsley is for damn sure enjoying it. I look at her now as she's trying to contain her excitement; it's funny.

"Mommy, I hafta be pretty. Can you fix my hair like yours?" she asks, poking her lips out.

"Maybe not exactly like mine, Sweet Pea, but I can make sure you look like a princess," I say, trying to convince her to accept the kid-size version of my current twist-out.

"I awready a princess. My daddy told me so," she says while twirling around in a Janie and Jack floral peplum dress with pink metallic flats.

"That you are, baby. Where are the two of you headed?" I ask although I am already aware that she will be meeting her grandmother for dinner.

"To meet my nana. Her said her is not a Glammie like my Glammie," she says, looking completely flabbergasted with a scrunched-up nose.

"I'm sure your Nana is pretty excited to meet you, Bumblebee," I say as I pull her hair into a simple top knot, leaving two spiral curls out encasing her face to give her just the right amount of sass.

Ms. Karen will almost certainly melt once she finally sees Kynsley in person. She surely did so once she cornered me in Kalyse's hospital room. As she was looking through pictures in my phone, she gasped at how much our daughters looked alike. In those moments of bonding, I prayed that baby girl pulled through. She has so much life to live and a strong support system in her mother and brother. They're always by her side. Every visit that's available for them, they are there. Wack ass Maxwell seems to only show his face when he knows, without a shadow of a doubt, that Kwame and his entourage will be in the vicinity. Good God, he's such a waste of a person. I worked it out with my coworkers to be nowhere around when he's present because it's taking everything in me to not hang him by his tonsils for even looking in my direction.

The ringing of the doorbell pulls me out of my thoughts. I glance around my living room to make sure my house at least looks presentable. God forbid one item is out of place, and it gives us yet another reason to not see eye to eye.

"Mommy, my daddy is here."

I smile as she smooths out her dress. I hate to admit it out loud, but she has picked up on some of my bad habits of insecurities. She's trying her best to be perfect in hopes of him never leaving again. Or maybe I'm just reading too deeply into the moment to really appreciate or admire the excitement my baby has for her father. "Mommy, are you going to answer the door?"

"Yes, Bumblebee, I am," I state, trying to hide the nervousness I feel. It seems that ever since we had that blow up in my kitchen, we've been tiptoeing around each other. But being that we are in an intimate setting, we have no other alternative than to engage for the benefit of our daughter. I have to catch my breath when I open the door. He's standing there, looking hella delicious, and if I'm being completely honest, Kwame has this dormant pussy on tsunami. *"Down, girl. Y'all are just co-parents. Don't fuck this up again,"* I think to myself.

"Hi, Daddy. I awmost readwy. Mommy did my hair pretty, so I wook pretty for Nana," my baby says with a smile, showing off her deep, chocolate dimples. And from the looks of things, Kwam is eating it all up.

"Hi, Princess. You will always be the prettiest thing on this side of heaven to me," he says with a wink, revealing a gorgeous set of beautifully straight teeth. "Hey, Gypsy, if everything goes well tonight, I was hoping you would be OK with me keeping her overnight."

"Oh my fucking word; I seriously need to get some. There ain't no way I'm about to toss him my panties because of a damn smile." I have to get myself together and fast. I'm sure I am standing here, looking like

somebody's lost puppy, battling feelings of yesteryear. I think Ana is absolutely right. I need to face my feelings of the past in order to truly get past my ghosts in my closet.

"Gypsy?"

"Oh. Yeah. Sure. Sure, it's no problem at all. I am sure she will enjoy it."

"Thanks. I also need to get ahead of the media and announce that I have a daughter. I know you take pride in having and keeping your privacy, but I would rather I announce it than to have the media dirty or portray an image of you and our daughter that is less than factual."

"Ummm... I guess that's fine. As long as it's strictly about our daughter with none of the narrative being about us."

"I'll have my publicist shoot you over an email so that you can scan over what we both feel comfortable with sharing."

"Works for me. At some point, we need to sit down and go over the schematics of our parenting plan. Maybe involve a mediator?"

"No need for a mediator. We can figure it out ourselves. I'll text you later to link schedules."

I nod my head as I see Kynsley re-enter the room. Baby girl is serious about looking good for her daddy and Nana. She's even pulled out one of her small purses my mother just thought she had to have.

"Behave for Daddy, Bumblebee. Be a big girl and use your listening ears."

"OK, Mommy. I be a big girl. Love you," she says as she smothers me with warm hugs and kisses.

"See you later, Gypsy," Kwame says with a wink.

"Her not Gypsy. Her is Mommy."

As I watch them go out to get loaded up to leave in the car, I am contemplating my feelings and what the hell just happened to me.

Kwame

Dinner with Kynsley and my mom was a success, not that I was expecting any different. It's just kids are so unpredictable, and well, this was my first time having her without someone she was comfortable with. I'm surprised Gaea even allowed this to happen with the way things stood between us. Regardless, I am grateful she did.

Kynsley is ever the charmer, and my mom has been eating it up. But that's Karen McCall for you. She's a beautiful, robust woman with a heart-shaped face, plump lips, stark gray eyes, a chestnut-brown bob, and a voice as dulcet as a songbird. Her calm and gentle demeanor is what I admire the most about her. It soothes the stormiest of seas. And despite what she has gone through, she is always smiling.

I'm not sure who is the most nervous between the two. But eventually they find a groove and stick with it. Kynsley stuck to me until she got a feel of the place, and then she slowly worked her way over to my mom. The only thing that was missing was baby girl and... Nah, I am not even sure where that shit came from. I can't even put effort into finishing that thought, because, well, we are attempting to reach a point where we are effectively co-parenting without the barriers of anger. Gaea and I are cool. Well, as cool as cool could be, being as the only conversation we've had was earlier during pick up for Kynsley.

"A penny for your thoughts, Langston?" my mom asks, interrupting my thoughts.

"Oh, it's nothing, love. Just have baby girl on my mind." I reply, revealing only half the truth. I can't possibly tell my mother that the woman I feel got away from me is haunting my thoughts. That I never truly got over her and the hurt that I felt. Nah, I'll stick to that half-truth any day.

"Yes, my heart breaks for her. It's so unfortunate that we even have to deal with this. I've been steadfast in prayer, so I know she will pull through. By his stripes and his stripes alone, she will be healed," she says, revealing only in her icy-gray eyes the sadness she felt. If it weren't for Gaea convincing her to go home and get some rest,

I'm sure when visitation hours hit, she would be there holding vigil by Kalyse's bedside.

"I agree, Mom. She is a beautifully strong little girl. Once she's home, I will do all I can to keep the both of you safe," I state, giving her hand a tight squeeze.

"Yes, darling, she is, and your little Kynsley reminds me so much of her," she says, changing the subject. "All of that spunk and sass in that little body is a force to be reckoned with. Nothing short of amazing. I'll have to thank Gaea for letting her stay over. She's such a well-rounded little girl."

"Yes, she is something special," I say beaming with a sense of pride. It's true. She's well behaved. During dinner, she only spoke when spoken to, she ate most of what was placed in front of her, and when she needed to use the restroom, she asked to be excused from the table. But after dinner, she was back to being my little chatter box. She wanted to know everything there was to know about her Nana. She tried playing coy with being around my mother, but she eventually hopped right into her lap and loved up on her as if she had known her her entire life. She talked so much that she tired herself out. She only stopped long enough to ask if we could stay at my mom's house. Once I agreed, she followed my mom to get her bath and to get settled into her aunt's room.

"How are things with you and Maxwell?" she asks, breaking me from my thoughts.

"Everything is everything, Mom. I remain respectful and ask only that he does the same. *Honor thy mother and father.*"

"Interesting. I'll leave you with this before I go to bed," she states as if it chokes her to say anything whether good or bad about the man she bared children with. "Don't let one scripture in the bible hold you hostage when there are many books in the bible that you can reach in and find freedom.

"Mom—" I start before she cuts me off.

"No, baby, listen. When you go into meditation tonight, take these two scriptures with you. 1 Timothy 5:8—*But if any provide not for his own, and specially for those of his own house, he hath denied the faith, and is worse than an infidel.* As well as Titus 3:10-11—*Warn a divisive person once, and then warn them a second time. After that, have nothing to do with them. You may be sure that such people are warped and sinful; they are self-condemned.*" Those should ease your weary heart, Langston. I've prayed for you so many times, baby, but this is one battle you are going to have to take head up and talk with God himself to release you. Now goodnight. I have a princess to entertain in the morning," she says and kisses my forehead for merit, leaving me to my own thoughts. I do what is already expected of me. I meditate. When my mind feels free, I drift off into a peaceful slumber that sends me straight into the world of Gaea.

Gaea

There are three things I know for certain, without second guessing my thoughts. One: everyone has an expiration date, as it was written by God himself upon creation. Two: Agape love is a love that surpasses all understanding. And last, but most certainly not least, wherever Kwame is, Maxwell is sure to be somewhere, slithering his trifling ass around.

The only solace I find in his being here in my space now is the fact that my little ballerina is currently sitting behind the nurse's station in my office. She's shielded from the filth that is him. I don't even have to say a word to Kwame about my baby being around him. It's as if for some unknown reason, he wants to keep her space as clutter free as possible, and whether he said a word or not, we both mutually agree that Maxwell is toxic. So there sat our little princess, in my office chair, being entertained by my co-worker and friend Jenn while I work and Kwame goes in to visit his sister.

He and Ms. Karen have become a Godsend since they've become ingrained in the world of Kynsley and I. I honestly feel as if a weight had been lifted off my shoulders once I had the support from not only my family but from Kwame and his mother as well. I honestly didn't realize I was carrying the stress and the burden of being both mother and father until I didn't have to any longer. I feel light. I feel free. I feel like myself again. I don't know how I will repay them, but I know that eventually, I will show my gratitude somehow.

As it stood, they are all in attendance to make medical decisions in regards to Kalyse's care. We are three weeks in to her being in a medically-induced coma. Today is the day that the doctors as well as Ms. Karen decided to wean her off of the machines. They're giving her a chance to fight on her own. As joyous as it is to bring her out, Maxwell has to ruin the mood of it all with his fucked-up ass attitude. It's taking everything in me to keep my stank face in check.

I swallow my thoughts as soon as Dr. Milo enters the room. Once he's seated, he begins to explain how we're going to gradually wake her up from the aforementioned coma. He continues, saying that it can take anywhere from six hours to a full day for her to completely wake up. The fight is ultimately now on baby girl if she's going to persevere or if she's going to let go.

While the doctor is talking, I can't help but notice Kwame is acting different with me. I can honestly feel when his eyes were on me. His eyes somehow always linger when I least expect it. Either he's softening up on me, or he's about to come for my jugular; I have no time to figure it out in that moment. Hell, I need to focus on what Dr. Milo is instructing me to do. But how can I when my body is burning with desire, and my mind is telling me to ignore his ass?

As luck has it, my vagina bottoms out the moment he licks his lips while eyeing me. I'm grateful I had the right mind to wear dark scrubs. He had my pussy crying a river. *"Girl, snap out of it!"* I think as Dr. Milo starts instructing me to shut off machines and to slow the medicines we were using to keep Kalyse sedated. Once she shows some improvement after waking up, she'll move to our step-down unit. The quicker this process happens, the quicker I can get control of my vagina, and the quicker wack ass Maxwell is out of my life. *"Good riddance."*

"Can you speed up the process? Flash has a training he needs to be at, and sitting at this hospital, waiting for y'all to do ya muthafucking job, ain't helping his time nor his speed," Maxwell spits out.

"You can't rush God's work. But we sure can show Satan out. Gaea, if you wouldn't mind calling security up to show Mr. Jacobsen out, it will be much appreciated," Karen states with finality.

"No problem, Ms. McCall." I bite back the urge to say 'my pleasure.'

"The moment that bitch picks up the phone to escort me out will be the day she regrets forever," he snarls out.

"See, what you not gon' do is disrespect her in my—" Kwame growls out.

"Oh, look who has some balls. When I'm around, you're usually mum. The bitch finally got to you and gave you some pussy and sweet talked you with the little bastard, and now you're disrespecting your father."

"Maxwell, it's time for you to go, now!" Karen shouts.

"Bitch, you sit yo' ass down and worry about this shit you let happen to Kalyse! I fucked up on so many levels when I nutted in you twice. I came back just in time for Flash! I got rid of the bitch once, but I didn't count on the hoe to be persistent. I saw then that Gaea was just like you, Karen. Looking for a come up—"

"Dr. Milo, can I step out…"

"No, bitch, you stay. Let's put this shit all on the—" He can't finish the sentence before Karen slaps the Jesus out of him.

"I'm going to step out so that I can get security myself," Dr. Milo announces, and I move to follow him, but Maxwell grabs ahold of my wrist.

"Sir, I'm going to ask you to please remove your hands from my arm," I say in a nice-nasty way. What he fails to realize is that I'm not afraid of his ass and his empty threats anymore.

"No, hoe, what the fuck is it gonna take to make your slut ass disappear again? A bigger payout? What? Those checks weren't enough?" he asked with an evil smirk.

"Disappear? Checks? What the fuck are you talking about, Maxwell? Are you telling me you knew about my God damn daughter? I know that's not what the fuck you're telling me!" Kwame growls out. The look on his face is that of death.

"What you're not gonna do is lie on me! I never cashed a single wooden penny of those checks! I didn't want blood money! You came after me when you found that I didn't get an abortion like you suggested and was gonna face Kwame! You said he didn't want anything to do with my baby and to keep…" I choked out.

"Maxwell, I know like fucking hell you didn't do what I think she is accusing you of! That's my seed, man! My baby!" Kwame yells.

"You were better off—"

"What is going on here!" Tobias inquires as he runs into the room.

Before anyone can react, Kwame has hopped over the bed and has Maxwell by the throat.

"Now you listen here, muthafucka! For the better part of fifteen years, I've sat back and stayed quiet about the fucked-up saga that is you. You got me so fucked up if you think I am going to continue to sit back and allow you to disrespect any of the women in my life. My sister, your God damn daughter, is fighting for her life, and you're worried about shit that has not a muthafucking thang to do with you. But that's not the icing on the God damn cake! You've released a God damn beast!" he growls as he tightens his grip.

"No, son, let me handle it. You and Gaea go and check on my angel. Now!" Karen demands.

"Let him go, Kwam. Let him go. I'll handle it from here with Mama K. Whatever it is, I got you, bro. You know this," Tobias coaxes.

Kwame lets Maxwell go, and he hits the ground with a loud thud. "Stay the fuck away from me and my family, man. I swear to God, I mean that shit," he spits out at him. "Gypsy, clock the fuck out! We got some shit to discuss!"

Leave it to Maxwell to fuck some shit up on what's supposed to be an exuberant day. Now I look foolish as hell on my job, and I have to explain some shit I swore I was gonna take to my grave.

Kwame

After dealing with Maxwell and his bullshit the other day, I needed a moment to myself to reconnect. It's becoming more and more apparent that I can no longer ignore his ass. He needs to be dealt with, and being silent has only enabled him to be unapologetically reckless. I have no one to blame for this but myself. That shit he said in Kalyse's room floored me. But what really got me is neither him nor Gaea said shit about knowing the other person. What the fuck was her aim?

When we stormed out of the room, initially, we were supposed to talk, but I couldn't even face her. Yeah, I made her ass clock out because, well, there were already too many muthafuckas in there, and I needed my publicist to play clean up. Now I'm here, doing this stupid ass interview with a woman I despise just so we can get ahead of the media shit storm. Because yeah, as suspected, a story is being shopped. I hope Maxwell isn't that fucking stupid to shop a story he played a hand in. But at this point, I can't put anything past him or anyone else.

"So Flash, we hear there's a new leading lady in your life. Would you care to share with your fans?" Stella asks, batting those awful false eyelashes.

"Why yes, Stella. There is this amazingly beautiful ball of energetic perfection that has recently become the highlight of my life. She makes every hard day easier and every cloudy day brighter. She's the best thing on this side of heaven. I don't think I've ever experienced a greater love," I say with a wink.

"Oh my, that's deep. Does this woman have a name?" Stella inquires. I know she wants the exclusive, but this is more for me than her. We need to get a handle on this. Her show is the quickest way to get the job done. The leak isn't about to get their payday. Not on narrating my life story anyway. As soon as I make this announcement, my team is informed to upload this gorgeous picture of my baby and me at one of her dance practices. She looks so angelic in her pink leotard. Ana took the picture of me crouched down, giving her a pep talk, as she held my face in her tiny little hands. Her smile was wide, bright, and innocently sweet.

"I can actually introduce you all to her. She's in the building. Would you like to meet her?" I ask, playing coy.

"Why yes. No better place to introduce her to the world than Stella's," she responds as the audience starts to whisper and look around.

"Give me a moment, and I'll go and bring her out." I walk backstage and grab Kynsley. She's dressed in a paisley shirt dress. The dress has a grosgrain trim and a navy-blue bowtie with subtle pleats. She's wearing her little brown riding boots with her hair in two big, curly ponytails. I have to say she complemented my outfit well. Being that I'm my normal dressed-down self in khaki chinos and a chambray shirt.

"OK, princess, we're on. It's time to work your magic," I say while tickling her.

"Silly, Daddy. Magic isn't real," she says while tapping my two nose rings. Immediately upon walking back out to the stage, the audience starts to "oh" and "aw," startling my baby, but like the true star she is, she quickly recovers.

"Ladies and gentlemen, let me be the first to introduce you to my little butterfly, Kynsley," I say as I sit down with her on my lap. I tickle her once more. "Kyns, go ahead and say hello to the people."

She straightens her back, pokes out her chest, and says, "Hello to the people. I Kynsley, and this goober is my daddy. I prayed for him." The audience starts to giggle, and I look over to Stella. She looks shocked but quickly recovers.

"Well, Flash, we definitely weren't expecting this. But what a wonderful surprise. Hello, Kynsley. How old are you?" Stella asks while looking down at my daughter and me.

"I am two, awmost three. Mommy said I gots to be patient," Kynsley says while smiling brightly, and just when I think she's done charming everyone, she winks at the camera and helps me out with the rest of the interview.

The day after the interview with Stella and social media blowing up, I meet with Tobias for our early morning workout session. Although he isn't an athlete, he still hits the weights with me from time to time. Tobias's nerdy ass went on to become a lawyer, graduating at the top of his class and eventually becoming an associate at his parents' law firm. Lately, I'm not sure if he's happy with that decision. But being typical Tobias, he rolls with it.

"T, how long did you know there was a possibility that I was Kynsley's dad?" I ask, hoping he wasn't another somebody keeping me out of the loop about my daughter.

"Honestly, for about two weeks. I was shocked that there was even a baby period. I've seen Gaea a few times, and I kick the shit with Ana all the fucking time. Ana is always on some other shit, so it doesn't surprise me that she kept this under the radar. But before I brought it to you, I needed to be sure."

"While I appreciate that, I still needed to know. Like, this whole situation is fucked up. How do you hide a whole muthafucking kid? Like, you didn't think while you were figuring shit out, I needed to know?"

"In retrospect, yes. But in that same token, we are talking about Gaea, not some jump-off, looking for a come up. It's something else there."

Thinking back on what he just said, I guess either way, being a mutual friend, he would've been in a fucked- up situation. Although it's a catch twenty-two, I have no doubt in my heart whatsoever that Tobias was gaging the situation to make sure it was in my best interest to know the truth while simultaneously protecting Gaea from a messy fallout. For that, I can't be mad, and I won't hold it against him. After all, he had been kept in the dark too.

"So the shit with Maxwell… How is that going for you? Are you cool, bruh?"

"I'd rather not talk about his ass. I'm gonna let the lawyers sort that shit out."

"I won't press you on it. Tell me about Ms. Kynsley. How are you handling that?" he asks, switching gears.

For the first time since finding out about Kynsley, I'm finally being honest with someone about my feelings. I go into depth about my fear of failing as her dad. For those very reasons, I explain that I have begun making strides to secure her future. Immediately after meeting her, I contacted my team of lawyers to set up accounts. I was so overtly excited about her future that I set up a LLC in Kynsley's name so that by the time she's eighteen, she can successfully run her own business and enjoy the fruit of her labor while still enjoying her college years. Upon her college graduation, I'll leave it up to her if she wants to buckle down and grow her company or if she'll like to sell it and start anew. It will only be my hope that she keeps her beginner business and start a second one all her own.

"Kwam, man, that's dope as hell. You are handling this news better than most. But on some real shit, you need to talk to Gaea about that Maxwell shit. How the fuck did she even meet him?"

"Shit, questions that need muthafucking answers. I'll get around to it, though. Soon."

"Cool things, just remember to keep a cool head. Again, she could be hiding some shit."

"Gotcha. Would you like to meet Kynsley? I pick her up from daycare today since Gaea is working a double tonight."

"Sure. What time should I meet y'all?"

"About seven or so. She needs at least a full hour to settle in."

"Ain't that some shit. A two-year-old winding down." He cackled. "I'll see y'all then."

Gaea

The aftermath of the shit storm that I not so affectionately call Maxwell is proving to be hell to get through. He's already managed to damage my personal life, and while that isn't great, I can roll with that. At that point, I still had my career to fall back on to bring me some sort of happiness. But now, his ass has managed to seep his poison into my professional life.

Since the blow up in front of Dr. Milo and the rest of the staff that was on duty, it had spread with a lot of fabricated stories throughout not only our unit but the entire hospital. While I ignore the whispers, I can't stomach the lies. I mean, what could I do besides take my petite firecracker of a friend's advice and say, "Fuck 'em. Let them talk"?

Jenn had been so clutch for that advice. It allowed me to buckle down and focus on my job since I also had to face the ethics board. When the relationship of sorts was revealed, I had to explain thoroughly that I had no personal relationship with the patient at all besides that with her brother. Some of which, I'm sure one or even a few of them, tried to shop around to the media. This was one time I had to be grateful coming from old money and having a child by a man who had a great PR team.

But even with that, I had to prove to them that my personal and professional life were two separate entities that held no bearings to how I would conduct myself professionally. Hence my busting my ass working doubles to prove a point, something I thought I was past when I cut the cord on my parents funding. *Point proven*, I think as I let out a deep and heavy sigh.

"Butterfly, are you even fucking listening to me?" Ana asked, clearly annoyed.

"Yes, Ana, I heard you. But I don't know what you expect me to say. Mommy is, well, Mommy. She's a prestigious, pretentious, materialistic socialite who is all about her image. Damn what we think or go through; it's all about appearances. We are unfortunately a part of that image and have been since we were born, so learn to be discreet with your dealings. There can only be one black sheep, and I fulfilled that role, so pick another lane, boo. Just think about it. I had to move away to escape her and her judgement. Well, that and well, you know, Aaron," I declare while mentally choreographing a musical arrangement to a song I couldn't get out of my head.

"Well, Butterfly, I have my dance company. I can't just up and move away. She's smothering me. She honestly can't be serious in thinking she can force me to get back with Miles with talks of pulling her yearly donation. I quite frankly don't give a flying, backward-country fuck about her blood money. I'll just have to find other avenues," she states while pacing the floor.

Her pacing is making me anxious, and it's taking all of me to not shake her and have her to sit down. "Have you talked to Dad? I mean, he is the one who convinced me to come back. He told me there was no valid reason I was hiding not only my life but dimming Kynsley's light when A, I am grown, and B, I was handling my business and had a degree to show for it. Not that any of that mattered, because I am a damn good mother. Good thing Mommy took to Bumblebee."

She looks out of the window for a few minutes before she turns around and says, "You know what? I don't give a damn if she takes me out of the will or disowns me. She will not force me into the life of bullshit and no orgasms."

"No orgasms?" I ask, raising my one eyebrow.

"No. None," she says, waving her hands dismissively before continuing on. "But on to more pressing news. What the hell is going on with you and Kwame? Why didn't you call me to whoop Maxwell's ass? And why is my niece charming the fuck out of America?"

"Dang, Ana, your mouth!" I say while rolling my eyes before answering her dismissively. "But to answer your questions, Nothing... Not necessary... And because she is her mother's child; that's why."

After sucking her teeth, she spits out, "No, bitch, you don't get to dismiss me!"

"Bug, I'm just tired. I'm both emotionally spent and physically falling apart."

"Yeah, alright, you get a pass today, but tomorrow? Oh yeah, bitch, tomorrow, you will talk," she says while laughing. "By the way, don't forget about Bumblebee's recital. I expect you to be there and helping."

"I'll be there with bells and whistles on!" I yell after her as she makes her way to my front door. "Lock up behind you!"

"Yeah, yeah, yeah! Love you, Butterfly!"

"Love you too, Bug!"

After showering and getting comfortable, I begin to work out some arrangements to a song. Not long after, I find myself getting lost in the melody, honing in on my chakras. My phone vibrates, interrupting the peace I'm in. As with everything else getting a portion of my time, I pick up my phone to see I have several missed calls from an unknown number and a text from Kwame. I ignore my anxiousness I feel about the unknown calls and open the text from Kwame.

Flash: Hey Gypsy. We need to talk, when will you be free?

I'm free now Kwame.

Flash: I mean without Kynsley being present.

I take a deep breath to check my attitude before I respond.

Being as she's out with my mother, again I am free. Where should we meet?

Flash: Ok. Open the door.

This dude really needs to know the importance of not showing up at peoples' houses unannounced. I storm to my front door, ready to go completely off on him for being inconsiderate to my time, my solitude, and my privacy. Yeah, it's been three years, but ain't shit changed about my space. He had the opportunity to talk to me when the shit blew up. But he chose not to. Yes, I get he was upset—hell, I was too, but to just pop up unannounced? Oh hell no.

As I open the door, every word that's about to slide off of my tongue is halted. There he stands, in a destroyed denim jacket over a gray hoodie with some fitted jeans and some wheat Timberland boots. He looks so damn good. I can't find my words, so I just stand there, staring at his lickable lips and his double nose piercings. My Gawd! I need to get control over my hormones.

Kwame

I know I'm taking a chance at getting cursed out by constantly showing up to Gaea's house unannounced. But well, fuck it. She has a lot of explaining to do. Being as she has a tendency to run or to sweep things under the rug when things get real, I'm no longer giving her the option to do that. It seems that for the last three years, everyone around me, including her, have been making decisions for me in regards to my daughter.

When we talked previously, she had ample opportunity to be completely forthcoming with everything, yet she remained silent. Taking that along with the manner in which she left, my threshold for trusting people is low, especially with women. Goodness, I know that since her, I have broken a lot of hearts. My motto is "Bed 'em and Dead 'em." I have no use in getting attached to anyone I can see no future with. I left my heart in the hands of one person, and she unfortunately dropped the ball. Today, I'm taking all that hurt and all of that anger that she'd gifted me and taking that power back. Today is the day I'm getting my just due.

"Kwame, you really have to stop showing up to my house unannounced. Not only is it annoying, it's also just rude," she says while opening the door wider for me to enter. When she closes the door and starts for the living room, mumbling some shit I'm not even trying to hear, I take that time to take her all in. Her face is free of makeup, and her hair is in a messy bun. She's sporting a pair of pink fuzzy socks, some tiny spandex black booty shorts, and what looks to be my sweatshirt from college.

"Yo, Gypsy, is that my sweatshirt?" I ask with a chuckle.

"Well, I guess it is," she says while blushing. "So what do we need to talk about that's so urgent you just had to show up unannounced?"

"Let's not play ignorant, Gaea. Help me to understand what went down at the hospital, and tell the entire truth this time, since you're having a hard time divulging everything."

She looks shocked, cuts her eyes at me, and shifts in her chair. She stares off for a bit, then she opens her mouth to weave the tale I'm not privy to.

"All this time, I honestly had no clue you truly didn't know about Kynsley until you were in my living room, engaging with her. But how could I come to you and vocalize that your father played a hand in neither you nor our daughter getting to know each other? That was a lot to swallow and cope with, so I suppressed it and carried on. It's better to take that gut punch and continue on than to keep looking out for the next one to hit."

"OK, Gypsy, I get that, but how was he even involved with all of this? Like, I'm not grasping the shit. You knew nothing of him, nor did he know anything of you."

All of this shit is confusing. When I finally went back to Brown State, I searched for Gaea. Like, I was literally stalking the girl and still came up short. I checked with everyone we knew mutually. I even went to Anais. But going to her was about as useless as a cow wearing an overcoat. All of her social media handles remained dormant until I eventually stopped checking at all until recently. Looking at them now, I notice she rarely posts anything at all, remaining mostly private. All that I seemed to find were mostly tags of her singing her soul out. My favorite so far is her singing a rendition of "Blackbird" by Nina Simone. Her voice was so raw, and her pain was evident. It's amazing. Vocally, she's strong, but according to Tobias, she was only using her voice as a form of therapy.

"Kwame, are you OK? You went silent there on me for a minute," she says, her voice filled with concern.

"Yes. Continue, Gypsy."

"Ummm… OK. So when I hadn't heard from you since before the combine, as I told you, I kept trying to reach out to you. I went to the gym. I went to the stadium, and I was constantly dropping by your apartment," she says, looking far off as if she's back in those moments. The sadness in her eyes has me longing to hold her in my arms. But before I can do that, I need to get to the bottom of this. Despite what we're going through now, I know in my heart that Gaea is mine. I knew it the moment I snatched Maxwell up that she was mine. But first, I need her to get the truth out finally.

"One day, I saw lights on in your apartment, and I thought finally I could get the weight off of my shoulders to share this load with you, my child's father. Even if you made the choice that I wasn't what you wanted, I knew in my heart that you would be there for Kynsley. I saw how you were with the children we volunteered with over Christmas our sophomore year of undergrad, so I knew we could raise our baby together. Only when the door opened, it wasn't you. It was Maxwell," she says while trying to hold herself together.

None of this was even making sense to me. Like, why was Maxwell even at my apartment unless it was during the time my family was packing up my life to donate some of my things to those in need after the draft? Things I no longer had a use for that would give some young kid from a single-parent household some hope. I see her shake her head as if she doesn't want to continue.

"Take your time, Gypsy. I'm not going anywhere, despite what is said or what was done," I say, trying to encourage her to continue.

She takes a sip of her tea and continues. "When I asked if you were around so we could talk, he completely ignored me. I thought it was strange, so I turned to leave. As I'm descending the stairs to head back to my car because it was obvious I wasn't going to get anywhere with him, I hear him say, *'If you came here to tell him you're pregnant, just get rid of the bastard.'* After I asked him to repeat himself, he again said to get rid of our daughter. I told him I wouldn't do an awful thing like that and left my information so that whenever you got the chance, you would reach out to me."

"I'm so sorry, Gaea—"

She holds up her hand, signaling me to stop so she could continue. "I just assumed he told you because a couple of weeks later, he sought me out, but this time, he came with money, telling me you wanted me to get rid of Kynsley. I explained I was too far along in my pregnancy, and even if I could, I would never give you or him the satisfaction. Maxwell said that I would be back begging for you to be a part of her life and demanding money. It was then that I made the decision to forgo reaching out to you in any way. I would raise our daughter in love and in light, despite you not wanting her.

"He gave me the 'yeah, whatever' shrug, dropped his information on my table, and demanded a paternity test be done once I had the baby. So boom, Kyns is born early, and again, here comes Maxwell because you were 'too busy' to come to submit a sample, so he did. It completely pissed me off because I had just read a news article about you being in Brownfield, doing a fundraiser for single mothers. Yet you would send your father to your sick daughter's bedside," she spits out and shakes her head.

"Imagine Maxwell's surprise when the test came back 99.9 percent that Kynsley was related to him. He stated you wanted nothing to do with her but would support her financially. I asked why you didn't send your hot-shot lawyers down her to relinquish your parental rights and completely be done with us as a whole, and again, he stated you didn't have time. It struck me as odd, but I was tired, Kwame—beyond tired at that point, and my focus needed to be on Kynsley. But every month, like clockwork, he would mail a check with a written letter instructing me to keep quiet. Checks that I never cashed, mind you."

We sit there, staring at each other in complete silence, allowing each other to take in the knowledge of what Maxwell had done. It cuts deep, knowing that my own flesh and blood could concoct a plan to hurt me in the worst possible manner. What I couldn't grasp is the why of it all. I doubt that by dealing with Max, I'll get any answers. None that would justify him playing a major part in my not knowing my daughter. I lost out on not only her, but a chance to clearly love her mother. The night we made love, I saw love there. I saw hope. I knew in my heart of hearts that she was my one. I gave her all of me and a promise to repair her broken heart. But I dropped that when I didn't push harder to reach her. I mean, Tobias and Anais were still kicking it off and on. I could've reached out to find her through T, but so could she.

"Gypsy, why didn't you reach out to me through T? I mean, come on. Neither of us used our resources. Like, did you not care about me at all?"

"I cared, Kwame. I just knew I didn't love you. Could it have possibly grown into love? Yes. I just felt indifferent. No matter how hard I tried, I couldn't bring myself to hate you. You gave me something beautiful," she said while giving my hand a reassuring squeeze. "Yes, I could've reached out to T, but in the midst of losing you, I was dealing with some other shit. So I shut down. My emotions weren't important; caring for Kynsley became my number one priority.

"I suppressed my feelings of neglect, hurt, and fear. By suppressing it, it became embedded into my soul, and I became angry. Not necessarily at you, but at everything. I walked around for three whole years, angry at the world. The hurt that I felt ate away at my heart and swallowed me whole. I mean, the entire three years I was gone, it consumed me. But knowing that hurt was in vain brings that hurt back to the forefront. Like another person was playing puppet master with not only our lives but Kynsley's life as well is a lot to swallow. I can't stand by and ignore Maxwell like you, Kwame. That's your deal. It's not gonna work for me."

I watched her succumb to her tears as I spoke as I sunk deeper into the couch. "You think ignoring him and 'letting things be' has been easy, Gaea? I've spent my entire life knowing my daddy didn't give a fuck about me until football gave me some clout, now knowing that this muthafucka has been standing in the shadows, maximizing his pockets off of my gift while hiding the fact that he was keeping me in the dark about my daughter. Disregard the fact that I have never received an apology. It was better to ignore him than to go against my faith and lash out, regardless of how I felt. Do you know what was beating me down? *Honor thy mother and father!*"

"I'm sorry. I didn't mean to imply that my hurt was greater." She cried even harder.

"Gypsy, come here," I say as I make a gesture for her to move closer to me. "I can't handle your tears, love."

"Kwam, it just hurts so bad." She sobbed, crawling into my lap.

"It's OK, love. What I do know now is that we will get through this together," I say, placing a tender kiss on her forehead and stroking her curly mane. "You are right. Had I gotten a handle on Maxwell and his convoluted bullshit, we wouldn't be dealing with this. You'd be my cliché bae, and I'd be your zaddy."

"It's not OK. But it will be soon," she says as she does a sort of sniffled laugh. As I look down into her big, coffee-colored eyes, it hits me. I can no longer live in anger or without seeing where the two of us can go. I wanted her in the worst way and not just as the mother of my child but as my woman—period.

"Gypsy, make no mistake in knowing that Maxwell will be dealt with stat!" I exclaim a little harsher than I want to. I feel her stiffened in my arms. "Relax, love," I say while giving her a chaste kiss on her lips. "There is something else I need to say."

"If you're about to tell me you have a secret family, save it. Let me rejoice in the fact that I can relax in the confines of my own home in the arms of a beautiful man and forget my troubles at least for a little while," she spits out.

"Woman, there is no secret family." I chuckle. "Beautiful, huh?"

She blushes as she speaks. "Yes, beautiful. So what is it?"

"I think you're beautiful as well, Gypsy. Go out with me so that we can make us official."

"What about Kynsley?"

"My moms can watch her. So before you say no—"

"OK."

"OK!"

"Yes, OK. Now, can I just lay here in your arms for a good little while and rest?"

"Yes. Rest your eyes, Gypsy."

I sit there for a moment, thinking of how different this could've played out but thankful that it's all working out for the greater good. As I watch her breathing even out, I come up with several different date ideas. It's not long after I hear her softly snore, I shift positions and drift off to sleep as well.

Gaea

After falling into a peaceful sleep with Kwame, I'm awakened by a fit of tiny giggles from my tiny terror and an austere inquisitive look from my mother. I roll my eyes as I glance over to see if he's still asleep. A soft snore gives me the confirmation I need. I place a blanket on him before I escort the two of them into the kitchen.

"So Gaea, is this what we're doing now? Allowing a man to stumble back into our lives, baring nothing but excuses?" she asks with enough edge to cut through a bowling ball.

I take a minute to look at her to make sure she's talking to me, looking around to show her how fucked up she has me in that moment. She somehow forgets her part in all of this. I clear my throat, choking on all the curse words I want to say, knowing it's unacceptable to curse your mother.

"You know, Mother dear, you lack a lot of tact and couth for a woman of your caliber. *This*"—I twirl my finger in the air to make a point of it being my home—

"is of no concern to you. Tread back on over to the country club and run someone else's life."

"Gaea, your mouth has always been something I've been less than thrilled about," she says while rolling her eyes. "You should be mindful of how you talk to me when I held you afloat when he walked out on you and my precious Kynsley."

Oh hell no. Her ass did not imply that she's the reason I held my life together financially. Truthfully speaking, the backing of a trust and busting my ass is what kept me going. Yes, my family lifted a helping hand with being hands-on with Kynsley. But I never took a dime from anyone, not even my father. Monetary "helping" was always refused for situations like this. She has been itching for someone to curse her out, and unfortunately, I'm not Ana, and pleasing her has never been my cup of tea. But I never expected it to be today, and it certainly isn't gonna happen in front of Kynsley.

"Bumblebee, please excuse Mommy and Glammie for a little bit."

"OK, Mommy! I go watch TV with Daddy," she says, eagerly skipping out of the kitchen, unaware of the storm brewing.

"Just don't wake him, love!" I call after her.

"Now back to you," I spit out, pointing my finger at my delicately dressed mother. "First things first, do not, and I repeat do not, under any circumstances, speak ill about my daughter's father in front of her. That is one of the quickest ways to get your visits cut short, and I don't give a country fuck how you feel about it."

"I didn't say anything bad. I was just stating the obvious. It would do you some good to recognize it before you're left pregnant and alone again."

"The obvious, huh?"

"Yes, the obvious. He's back and falling into the convenience of your lap. You're acting like a common whore! I raised you so much better than this."

"Whoa, and just like that, I am reminded why I can only stomach you in small doses. I thought maybe, just maybe, things would get better now that Kynsley is here, but no. I'm constantly being reminded of being forced into a life of seclusion because my mistake, which mind you, is a blessing, you see no problem with any longer because you flaunt her around daily like a God damn accessory."

"Forced!" She scoffed. "Hardly. When that scoundrel abandoned you, you jumped at the chance. I gave you and Kynsley the best life possible. No one gave a shit about you having a bastard child, because of your address."

"Listen here, Janet, and you listen damn good. If your ever in your life refer to my child as anything other than her God-given name, you'll be crawling and picking your teeth off the floor. Furthermore, I didn't jump at anything. *You* jumped into the picture when you realized having a grandchild was the new trend amongst your peers, but you only did that at arm's length. I was just a dark spot on your pristine image. It was Daddy that carried me and the emotions I was feeling. Now I love you, but what I won't allow is for you to continue to disrespect me, let alone in my own home," I say while stomping to the front door. "Now get the hell out before I say some things we will both regret."

"You and your sister are some ungrateful ass children, I tell you. I'll be by to pick Kynsley up for our hair appointment before her recital."

"No, Mother, you won't. You're more than welcome to come to the recital, but it will be a long time before you're able to be alone with her again," I spit out while opening the door.

"You can't be serious!" she spits out, completely flabbergasted.

"Oh, but I am! Have a good day, Mother," I say as I slam the door.

After I watch her 2018 G 550 Mercedes pull out of my driveway, I take a moment to catch my breath. I can't believe that after years of holding everything I felt for her in, it finally boils over and spills out. As I walk past the living room, I see that Kynsley and Kwame are none the wiser of the showdown I've just had in my kitchen. To clear my head, I hustle into the kitchen to get the makings of dinner out.

I just can't believe that woman. How dare she come into my home to disrespect not only me but Kwame as well. She doesn't know shit about shit except that we created our princess. Hell, if I'm being 100 percent honest, no one knows about Kwame and me besides the two of us—and well, Ana and Tobias. But that's neither here nor there.

Why can't my mother just be a normal mother? The type of mother that takes you to brunch and bakes cookies and shit? But no, that's too much like right. I'm instead blessed with a much prissier, prettier version of Eviline. Ugh! Such is life.

"Need any help with anything in here?" a deep, rich baritone asks, bringing me out of my thoughts.

"No. Well, yes. If you wouldn't mind setting the table, that would be a huge help," I say as I finish seasoning the salmon I'm preparing for dinner.

"No problem, Gypsy, but first, there is something I've been longing to do since you first opened your front door," he says as he rounds the island in my kitchen to stand in front of me.

"What-what is it that you wanted to do?" I stutter out, trying to get my hormones under control due to his closeness.

"This," he says as he leans in to kiss my lips. Just as I think the kiss will remain innocent, he pulls me flush against his chest. He deepens the kiss, sending my next series of thoughts into the universe, never to be spoken.

When I gasp, he takes that opportunity to slip his tongue in. Our tongues begin to do a sensual tango, bringing my nipples to a hard peak and the dam between my valley to spring a leak. I take a handful of his shirt and hold on to him as if I need his kiss to give me my next breath. Suddenly, he pulls back to nibble my plump lips. Dinner completely forgotten, I moan, giving him the clear clearance to do just what he wants with my body. He leaves a trail of kisses along my jawline until he reaches my ear.

I find comfort in his breath as I hear him say, "Don't believe a word she said. While your pussy is scrumptious, I'm after the heart that has held mine captive since you dumped blueberry tea in my lap freshman year." With that, he places a chaste kiss on my lips and smacks my ass.

"So you heard that, huh?"

"Yeah, every single word. Even the being sent away. Which explains a lot, boo, but I won't hold it against you. As long as I can stay for dinner." He chuckled.

"That shouldn't be a problem, being as I was making enough for three. Any special way you would like your salmon?"

"Nah, as long as I am here with you and Kynsley, I'll be more than satisfied," he says while finally setting the table.

Kwame

After back-to-back meetings today with my coach, PR team, and my agent, I'm beat, but I somehow have to gather together some strength to entertain my princess tonight. Who would have thought a couple of weeks back, I would be thrilled to pick up a miniature version of myself? Certainly not me. Hell, dealing with Kalyse is enough for me. While I love my sister with everything in me, this is a different type of love. So pure and tranquil. Tranquil? What in all hell? I'm getting soft out here. Yet that's all I feel as I feel myself getting excited as I pull up in front of a little, red, barnyard-style schoolhouse.

Knowing that Gaea took on the task of parenthood with grace did something to me. This further melted away my emotional turmoil of bitterness and anger. Despite how she felt about me, she didn't allow that to affect how our daughter viewed me. I found solace in the fact that even though I was gone longer than the month I gave her to end things with wack ass Aaron, she came looking for me to make things work. Three entire months of silence to allow me to do my thing in order to focus and secure my future. She pacified my ego while securing her own bag with a sick baby. That shit has my dick hard just thinking about it. Somehow, I need to show her my gratitude for raising a well-rounded little girl.

"Yo, bitch, you brought yo' punk ass up here to pick up my daughter?" Aaron growls out, interrupting my thoughts and killing my hard on.

I look over at him, chuckle, and continue my walk. There's no way in hell this muthafucka is talking to me, nor is he being this ignorant in front of my daughter's school. I haven't seen this dude since I caught him and this one groupie Yazmin in the gym, getting it on. Shit was mad wack on all levels. I could see why Gaea was over his fuck shit, having to deal with a cheater and his ego when his and Yazmin's performance was less than stellar. Well, to each his own. I mean, I honestly didn't see the significance of his being mad, because currently, neither of us had the girl.

"I know you hear me talking to you, bitch!" he says as he charges toward me.

"Aye, Aaron, I'm not gonna be too many more of yo' bitches. I'm only gonna tell yo' ass once to pipe down before I make you eat your words," I state with finality.

"My nigga, what you need to do is explain why you were fucking my girl and how there is even be a possibility she is yours!" he spits out while trying to rush me. In an instant, I grab his arm and pull it up his back while placing my forearm tight around his throat.

While getting within an inch of his ear, I whisper, "I don't give a fuck what you thought it was or what you think it wasn't. I *know* Kynsley Zora-Leigh Jacobsen is mine because when I was deep inside the silkiness of my pussy, I planted the universe in her womb. I hit it so good that mamas forgot who or what the fuck an Aaron was."

Feeling him getting angry and struggling to put up a fight, I continued. "I know she is mine because when she was milking the shit out of my dick, I touched her soul and produced greatness. Now when I let yo' ass go, take heed to the only fucking warning I'm ever gonna give you. *Stay the fuck away from my girls, or wake up dead.*

The choice is ultimately yours." I give him a forceful push and watch him struggle to get himself together.

I glance around to see that there's now a small crowd gathered around to watch us. Shit, I just promised my team I wouldn't do anything else that they would have to clean up not even forty-five minutes ago. How in the fuck am I gonna explain this shit? Lately, I'm always fucking up, but I'd do anything for my daughter and her mother. But God damn, I'm sick of bad press.

"Is there a problem here, Mr. Jacobsen? Mr. Williamson?"

"None. Would you be able to escort me to Kynsley Jacobsen's classroom?"

The pretty little redhead puffs her chest out and bats her false eyelashes before leading me to my daughter's classroom. Once I enter her classroom, all traces of irritation fade. I take a few moments to take in her surroundings as Ms. Cumberland gives me a run down on Kynsley's day. The joy on her face upon seeing me is infectious. Once she has her painting hung up, she rushes over to me and leaps into my arms.

"Oh my goodness, Daddy, I'm so glad to see you. TT Ana was gonna make me eat afairagainst for dinner," she says while scrunching up her nose.

I chuckle and kiss her forehead while saying, "Princess, we may not eat asparagus tonight, but you will eat a veggie with dinner. But to make up for it, I would like to take you to meet someone very special to me."

"Who? My mommy? I awready know her, silly," she says, falling into a fit of giggles.

Where the hell did that come from?

"No, but we are going to meet daddy's sister. She's looking forward to meeting my tiny giggle-box."

"OK, Daddy," she says as she wiggles down. "Let's go. Sydney's scary dad is here. He looks at me while I play with her. I not like it."

She proceeds to give him the cutest death stare I've ever seen. In that moment, she looks so much like her mother that it's scary. After collecting her things and having her say goodbye to her friends, we head out. When we look back, sure enough, Aaron is staring. The look in his eyes lets me know it's high past time to switch daycares and get my girls some much-needed protection.

Gaea

Trust me, it will take your heart

Trust me, it will break your heart, oh yes

It's so underrated

When we say and blame in love

Trust me, it will take

It will take all of it and break your heart, oh

Every day, we pray in love

To the god of it

But it's so good, so good

To be loved by you

Just as I'm about to get thick into the melody of "Loved by You" by Mali Music and Jazmine Sullivan, Jenn interrupts with her horrible rendition of what music should be. As she catches the hint that I need her to be quiet as I work through the rifts and runs, I make quick mental notes of what needs to be fixed. This show is one of need since the blow ups with not only Maxwell, but my mom as well, have me feeling off centered. My chakras were screaming to be realigned.

"Butterfly, get a hold of yourself. It's just Kwame, and it is just dinner. As much as he eats at your house now, and as much as you're over his place, this should be second nature!" Jenn exclaims.

"But things have changed. My body has changed. Hell, I have just been a chameleon with changing."

"Sometimes, change is just what the doctor prescribed."

"What if it doesn't pan out?" I ask somberly.

"But what if it does? Look, Butterfly, sometimes terrible things happen in order to make us appreciate and cherish the things God is giving us. We get a second chance to make it right," she says with a strong conviction.

"Hmmm, look at you with all that wisdom. You might be on to something."

"Wisdom that wasn't cheap. It almost cost me my life. If I can help someone else and save them a lot of heartache, then I will use the strength that I gathered to help as best I can," she says, blinking back some unshed tears.

"Jenn?" I ask, a little confused by her last statement. Ever since I met Jenn, she has been strong and focused. She's what most consider slim-thick with legs for days. As with Ana, she's constantly changing her hair, and she won't dare be caught without a face that's beat. What I love about her most is her spirit. I may have lost contact with all of my other friends, but Jenn is one I know I can't replace, nor do I want to. On days I wanted to give up, she would fly to me, pick me up, and curse me out until I felt better, which is why I find it strange that she's holding back her pain from me.

"So about the outfit you found in the back of your Madea's closet..." she says, switching gears.

"Jennifer, I resent that."

"Girl, you can't be out here looking like Tyler Perry's petite stunt double. No friend of mine is gonna be out in the world, embarrassing me for the culture," she declares while digging through my closet for a suitable outfit.

If I'm being truthful with myself, I would tell her that I am afraid to look sexy for Kwame. The feeling of what we share being only physical would crush me even more than us being apart ever did. When we were apart, it was easy to believe that the fear of being a father is what kept him away from me. But to actually be face to face and to feel a mental and spiritual disconnect? Man, that would be brutal, and I honestly don't think I'll be prepared to overcome those feelings.

My father, Theodore B. Lee Esq., would always say to watch a man's actions, and it will reveal the true desires of his intent for you. But I've been wrong before. Look at my choice for a partner in Aaron. That bastard showed me time and time again that I wasn't worth much of anything to him. He dogged me completely out. But I went with it because our families fit together. My heart didn't choose him; my damn mother did. Tsk… Seems she always has her hands in the most fucked up shit for the sake of an image, disregarding the fact that I'm totally unhappy. It's probably why I rebelled so much. Those two! Ugh!

But what has Kwame shown me as a man? Things with us as a unit are running smoothly. Aside from tonight, he always lets his presence be known. Even with his busy schedule, he always makes time to make sure that Kynsley and I have time with him. No matter how tired he is, he makes sure that we have dinner together as a family every other day when both of our schedules allow. At the dinner table, all seems well. We would talk about everything and sometimes nothing at all.

Then, there are the sunflowers he sends just to show he's thinking of me. So yes, things have been pretty sweet. But I can't help looking over my shoulder, waiting for the gloom to come, waiting to be surrounded by a sea of my tears, drowning in grief, wallowing in sorrow. No, I could never let that happen again. I'd gladly drink ten gallons of bleach first. So it's settled. I'll go on this date, but I will not fall for him.

"Sooooo since you're singing confidently again, do I smell another performance on the horizon?"

"Silly woman, I only sing to make myself feel good. Lately, there has been no need for me to do it. But I may grace the stage of Amour Noir again soon."

"Why sing?"

"Huh?"

"I'm asking why was singing your choice for therapy?"

"Oh, that's simple. It was the only time I felt free. I was able to get all of my feelings out without anyone questioning my sanity, questioning my thoughts, and questioning my entire being. Turned out I was pretty good at it."

"You ever think of doing it professionally?"

"I'm walking in my calling. This is just a hobby. Albeit therapeutic, there is no passion there. I lost that a long time ago. My passion is in nursing."

"Hmmm… Interesting… Just a thought. At any rate, what do you think of this?" she asks as she lays out items for my date.

"Perfect. Let's start on taming my mane."

Kwame

Visiting my sister and actually seeing her actively moving around brings me a sense of peace I honestly didn't think I would have. Seeing her interact with Kynsley as if they have been involved in each other's lives is dope on so many levels. Looking at the two of them together, I see my legacy—the hope for the next generation of Jacobsen's. My dedication and devotion for the two of them will forever be unmatched because I know within my heart of hearts that I'll stop at nothing to place the world at their doorstep and will die while trying to protect them from the cold, cruel world.

I've already begun the process of eliminating Maxwell from our lives for good. I honestly don't get a good feel on the situation of having him barred from the hospital as well as the stadium. The access codes and all things dealing with my life have been changed. According to my team of lawyers, he doesn't take too kindly the cease and desist letters we sent, asking him to forego business ventures that he had established, knowingly and unknowingly using my image, likeness, and my name. I figure we'll get some static, but I need to eliminate the cancer that's suffocating my life. How am I going to truly move forward as a man when I'm so used to letting a man walk over me and have a clear say so over my life when I wasn't being man enough to stand up and battle the toxicity that has kept me away from not only my daughter but also to truly grow?

Finding true independence outside of Maxwell's influence is proving to be great. I'm finding that I'm more focused in practices and weight training without having him barking down my neck about what I'm doing wrong and what I need to do to secure my future. Hell, I'm coming into my own as not only a father but also a son and a brother as well. The first thing I did was move my mother again and into a gated community. She had, by no means, lived in the hood, but I needed her to move closer to Kalyse's new private school. Mom was OK with the move, but that mouthy ass sister of mine gave me pure hell about making her appear weak in terms of her running.

She doesn't get that almost losing her, in the manner of which landed her in the hospital, gutted me. My sister, over the years, has become my source for securing a bag and wanting better for us. She won't become a statistic, and she for damn sure won't end up with a man like Maxwell. That shit is a hard no on so many levels. She's going to have a better life than I had when growing up. So having her mad at me for this moment in time is a teardrop in the ocean; besides, what can she do? Move back on her own? Nah, she can't, so for now, she'll have to deal with my choices.

"Kwam?" I hear a tiny voice say.

"Yes, baby girl?"

"I just wanted to say thank you, aight. Thank you for loving me and always being consistent with your love and care. But I also need you to step back."

I'm confused. So maybe I hadn't heard her clearly. I don't think she understands why I do the things that I do for her. I need her to have a better upbringing than I did growing up, so stepping back isn't really a viable option for me. But nonetheless, I push forward to ask, "What do you mean step back?"

"Kwame, I need you to be my brother and not my father. Yeah, Maxwell is a fu—screw up, but I am not lacking in any area of my life besides not having my brother. It was never your responsibility to take on the role of being my father, but I'm here to fire you from that position."

"I don't quite understand where this is coming from."

She looks at me with those big, brown, doe eyes and continues. "Going through what I'm going through has made me realize some things, and what I really need the most from you right now is for you to relax and just be my brother. Mommy did OK raising you, so allow her to do the same with me. You have a gorgeous little princess now, whom I adore by the way, but maybe you should redirect all of that energy in her direction. Judging from all that sass, you're gonna need it," she declares with a chuckle.

I think over what she said for a moment, and maybe she's right. I have always been more of a father to her, trying to make up and fill the cracks with what I was lacking in Maxwell as a father. Never did it dawn on me that maybe, just maybe, I'm not giving her the things she truly needs. She needs me, but not as a parental figure, but as her brother and her friend.

"I tell you what, baby girl. If you can give your new home and new school a fair chance with an open mind, I'd be more than willing to release the reins back into Ma's hands. But don't screw this up."

She twists up her face as if she's going to fight against the change that's gonna happen regardless of what we say. Then she starts to chuckle that turns into outright laughter. I must have been looking at her like she was crazy because she soon replied, "That works for me, Sir Daddy Brother."

"Then we have a deal."

For whatever reason, I'm nervous as hell as I pull up to Gaea's house. Like I'm a legit grown ass man and my ass is nervous. I'm talking butterflies and shit. No lie, that shit makes me feel giddy as fuck, but I will never admit that to anyone. Especially not Tobias's nosey ass. He'd never let me live that shit down. I can't put into words why I'm feeling this way; I just am, seeing as I put a lot of thought and effort into making this date one that she won't forget.

Knowing how big of an Alvin Ailey fan she is, I got us tickets to their show while they're currently touring. She's always speaking about the rich history of him shining light on African American participation to concert, dance, and making modern dance popular. I never understood her interest in the arts when she would stray away from actually being involved in the arts. None the least, she loves it, and I'm going to guarantee she gets to see the "Revelations" piece she used to talk my ear off about.

Afterward, we're going to one of her favorite restaurants, and while there, I want us to talk and truly reconnect, not as parents or lovers but as friends. I think it'll be best for us to go that route, being as we tumbled over everything else. I need her to see and to understand just how much she means to me. I want her to understand how much I've always cared about her. What I ultimately want to convey is that this shit for me is deeper than us being parents. Yes, my feelings magnified because of Kynsley, but nothing held more weight than what she's done for me. Our last night together, I truly felt like she was my one, but life and Maxwell truly gave us an ugly hand for any of that to manifest back then. But I'll be damned if we let kismet pass us over again. All of this has everything to do with her and how she makes me feel.

To show her I'm dead ass serious about us progressing, I've retired the fuck-boy uniform for tonight and dressed the part. I have to look like I'm a man about my business when it comes to her. There will be no half stepping. I step out of the Tesla and check my reflection on the car itself. Hell, I look rather dapper. The Tom Ford Sharkskin Wool Shelton suit is custom fitted to perfection, topped off with a crisp, white button-up with Cartier accents and black Giuseppe Spacey's on my feet. I had my barber hook me up this morning to shape up my beard and give me a fresh lining. Yeah, I look good as hell. Knowing what I know now about Gaea, I'm going in with a goal in mind. Woo the hell out of her and make it so no other guy can ever get close to her heart again.

Getting a little pep in my step as I make my way up her walkway, I'm eager to get our afternoon started. After ringing her doorbell, nothing prepared me for what's awaiting me on the other side of the door. There she stands, wearing a gorgeous, peach, crochet, lace, high-neck mini dress, nude Christian Louboutin 'so Kate' stilettos, and her hair blown out and flat ironed, hitting her right on her succulent ass. I look her over with no shame in my game whatsoever. My baby's gorgeous. When I get to her lips— oh my goodness, her lips! Those peach-colored lips make me want to make love to her mouth. Damn milk; Kynsley had done her mother's body good. My gawd, I want to forego our plans and make love to her right then and there.

"God damn!" I mutter, causing her to blush. "You look absolutely beautiful, Gaea. I don't think you know what you're doing to me, girl." Before I can help myself, I'm pulling her into my arms. I don't know if it's her pheromones or the light and flowery scent of her perfume that was making my dick spring to life, but I'm hoping and praying she doesn't feel the evidence of what her appearance is doing to me. As she wiggles in closer, I tilt her head and give her a chaste kiss.

"Thanks, Kwam. You don't look to bad yourself," she utters after we end the kiss.

"Shall we?" I ask, taking her keys and locking her door.

"Yes, my love. Yes, we shall," she croons while latching on to my arm.

My love? OK, I'll probe deeper into that later, but for now, I'll roll with it.

Gaea

"So where are we headed?" I ask as I quiet down the soulful sounds of some smooth jazz. Kwame glances over at me, giving me a small smirk.

Never would I imagine that I would be sitting with him again and not wanting to choke him. I mean, I knew we would get to the point where we were getting along, but I would have given you my last wooden penny if you would've said we would be out, nonetheless on a date. Hell, I know deep down, I still care for Kwame, even if it's only subconsciously. But I can't say that out loud after only sleeping with the man once. But I'll be damned if that once wasn't delicious. Just thinking about it has me shifting in my seat.

"Don't worry your pretty little head. Just know that your man is going to make sure you're more than satisfied with the outcome," he says, adding a wink.

"Satisfied, huh?" I mumble. He chuckles but doesn't answer me. He just turns up the volume as one of my favorite Nina Simone songs floats through the car, and I let her cover us in a comfortable silence. The song starts to get so good to me on our drive that I begin to sing along.

My baby don't care for shows
My baby don't care for clothes
My baby just cares for me
My baby don't care for cars and races
My baby don't care for high-tone places

As I'm getting caught up in the melody, I feel his eyes on the side of my face. I immediately start to blush.

"You have a beautiful voice, Gypsy," he says.

"Thanks," I mumble as he parks the car.

"You should use it more," he states, and before I can open my mouth to object, he's out of the door and making his way to my door. We make our way to a theater that appears to be closed. I glance over and see him become nervous. Thinking that maybe he has our days mixed up, I turn to assure him that everything will be OK, but I'm startled to the doors opening and the lobby being filled with calla lilies and sunflowers. He blushes and leads me on into the theater.

"I wanted to do something special for you without looking like a complete sap. I'm praying that my efforts are not in vain and that your favorite things haven't changed one bit. I brought you here today so that you and I could have our very own viewing of 'Revelations,'" he murmurs out after placing a kiss on my forehead. Immediately, tears spring to my eyes. In this moment, he has shredded every single doubt I had about our connection being nothing more than physical.

"Don't cry, Gypsy. Just know this is a small token of my appreciation for you. Not only for who you are to Kynsley but for what you are to me as well," he states.

Although we have the theater to ourselves, he leads me up to the balcony to be seated. As we're being seated, it finally hits me that outside of whatever we have going on physically, Kwame is genuine and thorough with his care for me. He remembers the small things about me, like my love for the arts as a means to escape the stressors of life or that sunflowers bring me a type of peace I can't fully explain, and sometimes, I just need you to be present but not in my space. It's like he gets me and all my weird quirks. It's for these reasons that not only am I happy to have him in Kynsley's life, but I'm excited to have him as a part of my life also.

As the dancers move around on the stage, I can't help but stare at my man. Knowing he went through all this trouble for me makes me want him in the worst way. I glance around the balcony to see if there are any cameras before I make my move.

"Gypsy, why are you moving so much? Do we need to mo—"

Before he can finish his question, I straddle his lap, kissing him with a passion I feel all in my soul. As he takes control of the kiss, I make quick work of freeing him. Breaking off the kiss, I drop down to my knees and lick the length of his shaft. My eyes widen at the sight of the beautiful masterpiece in front of me. I mean, I knew my baby was packing, but damn I sure as hell don't remember it looking this good. The thickness and length make my salivary glands go into overdrive. Then, in one quick move, I immerse his scrumptious head into my mouth. He lets out a moan of pleasure, and sure enough, Kwame brings his hands to my hair and tightens his grip.

"Oh shit, babe!" Kwame bellows out.

That takes me over the edge. Nothing brings me more pleasure than pleasing my man. If I'm being completely honest, nothing gets me more excited than the feel of his swollen head on my tongue. As I run my tongue up and down his thick shaft, I glance up at him and wink. I can feel my pussy get even hotter and flow with excitement with each pulse I feel in my mouth. But this isn't about me; this is about pleasing my man. OK, I'm lying. This is just as much about me as it is about him. I love the thought of having him in my mouth. The shit feels powerful. If I'm not careful, I can cum just from fellatio.

Having lubricated his dick enough with my saliva, I use my left hand to pump away, alternating between that and my mouth, creating a suction that rivals my pussy. Seeing he's thoroughly enjoying my mouth, I let out a moan of pleasure to show him how much I enjoy pleasing him just as much as he enjoys receiving. He tries holding off as much as he can, but he's no match for me. I gently massage his package and take as much of him in as I can. I let off a low hum in my throat, and he grips my head tightly so that he can continue fucking my mouth.

Before I know what's happening, Kwame yanks me up and rips my panties off, bringing me down on his dick. He captures my mouth and makes slow laps around my mouth.

"If I didn't already love you before, I sure in the hell love you now." He grunted in my ear. "Ride daddy, baby."

Hearing that pushes me further over the edge. I start working my hips like I'm an extra in Nelly's "Tip Drill" video. I clench my walls, knowing I'm heading over the edge, and I feel him matching me pump for pump.

"That's it, baby. Show me this pussy is mine," Kwame growls.

"I'm about to cum, baby!" I scream as I feel the tell-tale signs of fire in my stomach.

Kwame grabs on to my hips and guides us into Oscar-worthy orgasms. "Oh shit, baby, I love you so much," I say as I'm coming down.

"You love me, huh?" he asks as he looks into my eyes. "It's OK, baby. Daddy loves you too. Now let's get home so that I can show you how much."

Kwame

A few days after our date, and I'm still coming down off of the high Gaea gave me. My crazy ass had the audacity to admit I love her, knowing she'd freak out at any mention of emotion. But surprisingly enough, Gaea admitted she loves me herself. That, without a doubt, has a brother feeling good. But tonight, all thoughts of us would have to be pushed to the wayside. My baby is having her first dance recital, and I'm definitely the textbook definition of a proud dad.

This moment is even more special because Kalyse is in attendance with us. They released her from the hospital a few days prior, but rather than rest, she decided she needed to come and see her mini me perform. She's here front and center with her "Proud Aunt of Kynsley" shirt on. It seems as if my baby has won the hearts of all the women in my family. My heart swells with pride and love once I see the bond between my two favorite mini's. It seems as if Kynsley were the catapult in Kalyse's healing.

It came as a complete surprise that Gaea's mother, Janet, greeted me with open arms. Her father, Theodore, on the other hand, had always been warm and inviting.

"Hello, son, it's nice to see you in attendance tonight," Theodore says.

"Likewise, Mr. Lee," I respond while extending my hand for a shake.

"Cut out all that Mr. Lee business. Ted or Dad works just fine," he says, giving me a knowing look.

We continue with small talk before I introduce them to my mother. Shortly after, Gaea joins us, and although the tension between her and her mom is thick, it's actually pleasant conversation. Sensing her anxiety over her dealing with her mom tonight, I pull her in for a tight hug and a chaste but passionate kiss. I need her to remember that I'm here for her, regardless of what's transpiring between her and her mother.

Just as we make it to our seats, the lights are dimmed, and Anais comes out to thank everyone for coming out to Creative Expressions Dance Studio annual recital. As she exits the stage, the lights dim, and the musical musings of Deee-lite's "Groove is in the Heart" begins to play. My heart starts to smile when out comes my daughter in a fuchsia foil printed spandex and sequined metallic mesh leotard that has an attached top shirt with a spandex binding strap. To top the look off, she has a separate chiffon tutu, a black sequined belt, all embellished with more sequins and rhinestones, and a big fuchsia bow on her left shoulder. Her hair is done in an up-do in the shape of a bow instead of the traditional bun all of the other little girls are wearing. Yeah. my baby's extra, much to the dismay of Ana, but she rolls with it. I guess she can sense my excitement of just being a new stage dad.

Kynsley comes out with a big ball of energy, doing her very own rendition of what I have come to know as a jazz walk. The music picks up, and she starts to shake her hips in tune with the beat, doing a jump, clap motion. She starts doing chassés across the stage, leading into miniature pirouettes. Watching my baby dance and glide around up there brings an unexplainable sense of pride. I mean, granted, I know she's only almost three, but my goodness, she's an absolute natural up there.

Upon them ending the dance, I do what any self-respecting father would do. I stand up and hooped and hollered like she had just won a Grammy for best choreography. I'm cutting a fool so bad that my mom yanks me down. Eventually, I settle down and continue to enjoy the rest of the recital and rejoice in every part Kynsley has.

At the end of the recital, as I'm seeing my family off, something in my gut feels as if something is all off. When I saw Gaea rushing toward me, from the look in her eyes, I know that I'm right.

"Baby, please tell me you have Kyns!" she chokes out.

"No, I haven't seen her since she skipped backstage with the rest of her class to change clothes."

"Oh my goodness, babe. Kynsley! My baby!" she screams, and she bursts into a fit of sobs.

"Let's check the building completely."

"I have! Call the police now!"

Gaea

It seems as if my life's sitting at a complete standstill. I'm praying for a reprieve, praying that I'm either dreaming or that someone's playing a sick joke on me. This just can't be life. My baby doesn't deserve this—hell, I don't deserve this pain. Poor Kwame, my boo was such a proud dad tonight. A little over the top, but who can blame him? Our Kynsley is something special. My parents— well, rather my mother—was pleasant this evening. My daddy is always cool; it was his wife that was extra.

My parents... Maybe they took Kynsley with them. I quickly dial my mother's number.

"Hello?"

"Mom, it's no longer funny. Where is Kynsley?" I spit out.

"Gaea, whatever do you mean? Where is Kynsley? I don't have her. You do remember you throwing me out of your house and barring me from seeing my princess!" she bellows out, her voice laced with ice.

"Look, Janet, if you don't have Kynsley, then I guess I must be crazy."

"I mean… well from the looks of things…" she says as I hear my father in the background, mumbling something about her atrocious behavior before she corrects herself. "Look, Gaea, I truly have no idea what you're talking about. Your father and I are only a few minutes away. We will be there in ten."

It doesn't even register or fully set still in my brain what my mother has said. All I heard was she doesn't have my daughter, and she's for sure missing. It takes everything in me not to scream and cry. I know if I have any luck in getting my baby back in my arms, I need to think clearly and suck up my emotions. I think back to the last time I saw her. She was so happy and skipped all the way back to the dressing room with her dance troupe.

I look in the direction Kwame is, and from the look on his face, his efforts are fruitless as well. My feet feel like concrete as I make my way to him. Before I can get a word in, he silences me, instructing some guys to secure the building. Once the building is finally secured, I hear Kwame unleash a different side of him. He's sort of like a lion untamed, and no lie, if we were in a different setting, that would have surely turned me on. But in this instance, he's ferociously protective of his tribe. He's a hurt father, looking to have his daughter back in his arms at all costs. From his actions, I learn that apparently, Kynsley and I have a security detail—one that isn't very good if our daughter still came up missing.

"How in the fuck do you lose sight of a two-year-old? A two-year-old you're being paid to protect?" he barks. "You know what? That question has to be rhetorical, because there is no way in hell I'm staying here without my daughter. All you muthafuckas are fired. I swear, on everything that I love and as sure as God raises the sun in the morning, if I don't find my daughter, y'all will pay for this shit with your life."

I guess I must have looked scared in that moment or like I would flee away from him, because he inches closer to me and says, "Gypsy, don't leave my sight! Stay right here until I take you to my house. Are we clear?"

I quickly nod my head as he kisses my forehead.

Just as he turns away from me, my parents enter the building. I don't want to talk. I don't want to answer the questions. But it looks as if they aren't going to come anyway. Kwame and my dad are speaking in hushed tones, more than likely about their course of action outside of help from the police. The more I sit there, the angrier I become. I silently rack my brain to figure out who would do something so cruel to us. Who would honestly snatch Kynsley that isn't family? It can't be a crazed fan of Kwame; that just seems so farfetched.

My mind shifts in a million different directions a million times, and at each turn, every single nook and cranny, it always goes to Maxwell. His smug ass face is permanently burned into my psyche. The more I see him, the angrier I become. I'm getting so bad that I'm literally shaking. I struggle to make sense, to make any of this make sense in my head. This whole situation makes me sick. Here I am, forcing myself to believe that he can't do something this foul. That he can't be this horrible to his granddaughter. I begin to hyperventilate. It's becoming hard to breath. Just as I place my head in my lap, I hear my mother ask for a moment with me. I can't deal with her in this moment. A woman with no maternal bone in her body can't imagine the pain I feel.

At least that's what I think. But before I knew what's happening Janet Lee has swooped me up into her arms, and just like that, I feel myself calm down. In that moment, whatever ill feelings I had toward my mother, we put to the side. She's giving me exactly what I need. Strength. Silence. Unconditional love. Yes, my resolve is broken, and I'm able to lighten my true feeling.

Once the police come in and do their routine line of questioning and sending out the Amber Alert, I can't stomach being around people any longer, but I know I can't face going home without my baby.

"Baby, I'm ready to go. I can't do this anymore. Please just take me to your place," I plead.

"Gypsy—"

"No, baby," I croak, throwing myself into his arms. "Please, I need to go before I fall apart." He looks me over, checking to see if there's anything else I need. But no, there isn't a single, solitary thing I need in the form of these people. All that I know was that I need him. I need to be away. I need everything to sink in. I need him to be everything he's being now. My strength. My protector. My man.

"OK, love, give me a minute to wrap things up," he says, squeezing my hand and walking toward my father. I decide I'm not giving anyone else a moment of my time. I look over to the two men that I love, and retreat to my sister's office. In there, I completely break down.

I finally let out the most gut-wrenching, ear-shattering cry. I don't care in that moment that someone can hear me. I don't care that I'll be perceived as weak. All that I care about is my baby and knowing where she is or even if she's safe. I'm getting to the point where I can't breathe, full-on ugly crying, hoping this will make me feel better so that I can get up and face the world tomorrow with the strength of ten thousand armies. Before I know what's happening, I feel the energy in the room shift. I smell his warm, masculine scent and feel his muscular arms lift me up off the floor to hold me in his arms.

"Let it out, my love. Let it out. I promise, you we will get through this and get our baby back," he croons, and from the look in his eyes that are now an onyx-colored abyss, I know he means that from the bottom of his soul.

Kwame

Seeing Gaea break down is about all I can take before I go and rip the security details' heads off. I know in my gut something isn't right. When I saw Aaron in the building, I should've followed my first mind and not let Kynsley out of my sight. My baby said herself that he made her feel uneasy. Aaron has to be completely out of his mind if he thinks I'm going to let him get away with this. After breaking down the entire situation from college on, to Theodore, including the fight, he makes cohesive efforts with me to assure that whoever has my daughter will pay for it. My team of lawyers along with Theo were ruthless in the courtroom, and given the severity of the situation, I'm more than impressed. My celebrity has us posted all over every news outlet you can imagine. With that being so, despite my wishes not to, Gaea has decided, along with our team, that we need to speak with the public.

All I want right now is peace; I need that in order to stay strong for my family. I make it point to have complete tunnel vision. For right now, all I care about is getting Giselle comfortable and getting my baby girl home. It has completely shattered my already bleeding heart when I hear her cry out from Anais's office. I want to break down then, but what good will that do for us? If I break down, who will be there to carry us through? Instead, I break everything down in my head as if I'm running a football drill. Everyone and everything is disposable. They're essentially my opponents, and nothing is going to stop me from getting to the end zone.

Thank God Ana and Tobias come in at the moment they do—because security is about to pay for my heartache and Gaea's tears. At any other time, the two of them disappearing and coming back disheveled, but for right now, whatever they have or don't have going on will have to take the backburner. I'm grateful for them jumping in the manor they did so that I can get to my baby.

*****

"Baby, can you come to bed? I just need you to hold me until I fall asleep." Hearing her weak voice brings me back into the moment. Seeing her like this makes me want to give her the world twice over just to restore the peace, harmony, and light back into our world. But in that same instance, it makes me angry all over again. I turn from looking out my floor-to-ceiling bay windows over the twenty acres of land, hoping to find some answers in the beauty of it. I quietly make the trek over to my California king bed where she's currently lying. I climb into the bed and pull her on top of me where I can gently rub her back. As I soothe her, she blesses us with her beautiful voice until we fall asleep.

The   blood   that   Jesus   shed   for   me
Way   back   on   Calvary
The   blood   that   gives   me   strength
From   day   to   day
It will never lose its power

The next morning, I awaken to the wonderful feeling of warmth around my shaft and a melody of soft moans. I want to hold out because the both of us are in a fragile place. I don't want to feel bad for making love to my woman while our daughter is missing, but with one clench of her vaginal walls and the angelic look that's on her face, and I'm a complete goner. I pull her mouth down toward me and kiss her with all of the love I have for her down in my soul.

I alternate between slow laps and wild, untamed laps before flipping her over and driving into her so deep that I swear I find the eighth wonder of the world. As I pull out, I slowly savor every sweet sound and become enthralled in the silky, velvet feeling of her love canal. It's an incredible sensation, and my strokes became faster and more urgent. She's practically lifting herself on the bed, matching my strokes pound for pound. I rock into her until I feel her pussy begin to contract around me, and I know he can't hold out any longer. Just as I feel her juices pool around me, I pour all of my seeds into her warmth, completely filling her womb. As we struggle to catch our breaths, I pull her into the warm cocoon of my arms.

After a few more rounds of lovemaking, we decide to shower separately so that we can make it out of the house to the press conference in hopes that someone will come forth with some information on my baby. After stepping out of the ensuite and finding the bedroom empty, I look out on the balcony to find her in one of those fancy ass chairs that my mother convinced me to buy with a mug full of blueberry tea. I should've known I would find her here. For whatever reason, the rain relaxes her and allows her to think freely. Whatever that means.

I quickly pull out my phone to capture her in this natural state. It's not long before I hear a beautiful melody of music flow from her lips, calming my spirit. I catch her eye, and she motions for me to join her. As the song ends, we sit in comfortable silence until she speaks.

"Do you know why I'm growing to love sitting out here?"

I shake my head no.

"It allows me to process my feelings, and lately, they've been wrapped up in you."

I try to speak, but she stops me.

"No, let me finish. I've come to the very real conclusion that I love you."

I turn my head to look at her, completely taken aback.

"Yes, you heard me right, Kwame. I'm tired of running from something I know is good for me. I needed you to hear it from me when we aren't chasing an orgasm. Kynsley deserves to have the both of us, which is why it's imperative that we find her. Safely. Fear ran me away before, but this time, the three of us have to grow deeper in love. Promise me that no matter what happens, you will be right by my side."

I'm at a loss for words, and I can't vocally express how I feel, so I take her to my bed and show her everything my mouth can't say.

Eventually, we get dressed and go on over to do the press conference. It's the events after the press conference that have us at odds. We're currently not speaking. We enter Gaea's home to grab a few things since, currently, my house is the safest and free of the media. But I just can't shake the energy shift once I voiced to the police how I think Aaron is behind this. If not behind it, then he has something to do with it. It pisses me off because she isn't trying to hear anything I'm trying to say. Her brain is fixated on the fact that it can very well be Maxwell. I'm not counting him out, but hell, I'm not willing to put all of our eggs in one basket.

"You're either blind or completely naïve to the fact that Aaron is more than capable of doing something like this.

If you aren't willing to have the police confront him about this, I will. Actually, it doesn't matter now, because they are, and that's final!" I bark out.

"Did you just call me stupid, Kwame? Just because I won't accuse a person I knew and loved of something as serious as this doesn't make me stupid. I'm just looking at all of the facts!" she yells back.

"And the fact of the matter is that the 'love' you feel for him is blinding your stubborn ass to the fact that our daughter may very well be in his arms," I say as I look out the window, disgusted that we're even having this conversation.

"You know I wasn't saying I love him," Gaea defends.

"You didn't have to say it. The shit was implied, Gaea," I spit out.

"Fuck you, Kwame!" she screams at the top of her lungs.

"Fuck me? Fuck! Me! Great! Just great. I'll talk to the police again myself and share whatever else we come up with. I'm done with this back and forth shit with you. I'm done with this! Have a good day, Gaea!" I say as I make my way to the door.

I continue to my car, angry as hell that she can't see Aaron for the snake he is. I can't keep going through the motions with her. I laid my heart out to her, and she continuously spits on it. That shit is draining. I can't go back to the man I was with her in undergrad. As soon as my daughter is found, I'll handle things with her once and for all, but for now, that shit is taking the backburner. Finding Kynsley is key; the rest of this shit has to take the backburner.

Gaea

After getting no solid lead on where Kynsley can be and no signs of Maxwell, I'm completely at a loss. My only other option is to meet with Aaron since Kwame is convinced he has something to do with my baby's disappearance. I'm not so sure about that, being as I've told Aaron that there's no possible way Kynsley is at all his. Never mind the fact that we weren't intimate for at least a month and a half prior to my being with Kwam, but also due to the fact that DNA has successfully proven that she is Kwame's. So yeah, Kwame is being a complete lunatic. Aaron is a lot of things, but a kidnapper? Nah, I can't see that.

Needing to clear my head and get some air, I decide to drop by the hospital and check in with Jenn. Having a late lunch with her will ease my mind.

"Hey, boo, hey! How are you holding up?" Jenn inquires while engulfing me in a much-needed hug.

"Not good, love. Not good at all. I just want my baby back safe in my arms and in my home," I croak out.

"I know, babe. How is Kwame holding up?"

I shake my head and defiantly say, "I wouldn't know. We aren't speaking beyond tag teaming the police department for answers."

"Hmmmm..."

"What, Jenn? Are you about to give me some of the infamous Jenni wisdom?"

"I would but—"

As she's about to finish her next thought, I lock eyes with a beautiful woman. She looks to be about five feet six without her stilettos. The woman sports a blonde pixie cut, round, tortoise shell eyeglasses, and a stark, white cat suit under a blue blazer, and she's wearing red shoes that match the red lipstick she has on her lips and nails. She looks vaguely familiar, especially along the eyes. There aren't that many African Americans that I know with gray eyes.

Nonetheless, I draw a blank, and I can't recall where I know her from. At the same time, as I'm getting ready to speak to break the awkwardness of the moment, those gray eyes go cold, and she mouths, "Checkmate, bitch!" Then she struts off to meet her awaiting party.

Although I'm confused by the interaction, this confirms that I know her from somewhere. Whilst trying to figure out what has just taken place, I see that Jenn caught the entire interaction, so I ask her if she knows her. She goes on to explain that her name is Lisette Toussaint, and she's always a constant figure around the hospital. She isn't aware of any titles she holds but states that she's problematic for anyone she encounters. Jenn warns me not to get on her bad side, because it can be detrimental for my career in nursing. It looks to be too late for that warning. As I follow Jenn out to the hospital staff entrance, I send out a text to my daddy as well as Tobias to check this woman out. I can't shake the gut feeling that whatever they find, I'll know that Kwame is right.

Ana joins us for lunch, which is refreshing to say the least. I have missed out on the closeness of my girls while drowning in my misery. I try to keep a low profile because of Kwame's celebrity, but it's hard to process that I need to stay in seclusion to realign my chakras now that my daughter is missing. Even with that, I can't help but notice Ana's stank attitude, but for now, I let it slide. I have too much on my mind to deal with Ana's tantrums.

Is it Kwame's fault that our daughter is missing? In reality, no. But had we not been so caught up in one another at her recital, then Kynsley would still be in the comfort of her own home. Then he made this big deal about my being blind and naïve about Aaron when that can't be further from the truth. He hurt my damned feelings. So who else can I blame in this moment other than him?

I'm reminded of his "guilt" every time I step out of the house, and paparazzi is right at my doorstep, bombarding me with questions. None of these things would have happened if I would have stayed tucked away. But no, I just had to get my life back—a life that wasn't designed for a spirit like Kynsley.

"You can't keep blaming yourself or him, Gaea. He's hurting just like you!" Anais says.

"How would you know?" I spit out.

"Because I actually talked to him, unlike you. He's sick out of his mind drowning in grief. Think about it.

One minute, you're single and living your life, completely kid free, mind you. Then in an instant, you find that you are a father, and you're knee deep in daddy mode, enjoying every single God damn moment until suddenly, it's snatched away with no warning or explanation. Further adding to his grief is knowing that the woman he loves is blaming him for your missing daughter and is just too damn blind to see that she is blaming the wrong somebody."

"Love? Ugh, hardly." I scoff.

"That's all you got from that? After every fucking thing I said, that's all you took from it?" Ana asks, suddenly enraged. "You know, I knew you were stubborn, but I never took you for stupid."

"Excuse me?" I ask, stunned that she's even talking to me like this. I look over at Jenn to see if she'll step in, but it seems she's in agreeance with Ana, so no, she isn't going to step in either.

"You've been excused long enough! Fix your shit! You're not the only damn somebody hurting. Hell, she is only my niece, but that shit gutted me! Stop blaming that man when he is not the only one that has baggage! It was my studio, and hell, I don't see you blaming me for not one single, solitary thing. Yet you sit here all smug, just like Mama, blaming that man when all he's ever done was love you despite what you dropped at his doorstep! I'm gone because I can't stand to look at you any longer." She reaches in her bag and tosses enough money on the table to cover the bill plus the tip and storms out.

Kwame

It has been a few days since I've laid eyes on Gaea, and although I still feel some type of way, I can't help but to miss her. She has only been in my space for a few days, but it seems as if her scent is embedded into every crevice of my home. The more I lie in this bed, the more the sweet smell of sunflowers tickles my nose. It's in my sheets and my pillows—hell, even in the T-shirt I'm wearing. It seems as if no matter what my housekeeper does, there's no getting her scent out of my home. Not that I want it to go anywhere; the shit is just annoying, knowing that I can't have her right now. I can't begin to understand and sympathize with her when my baby girl is gone. Like the shit doesn't involve rocket science. Why can't she see that Aaron is behind the disappearance of Kynsley?

I have worked it all out in my head, and no matter how I flip shit, it always comes to Aaron. It makes perfect sense. He's always lurking in the shadows of Gaea and Kynsley. Kurt, a member of my security team, made sure to let me know he had been snooping around their neighborhood. I want so bad to continue being mad at her, but how can I honestly be? She isn't privy to that type of information, so she can't possibly know that this nigga is completely out of his mind like he's dived head first into a cesspool of crazy. I don't see the connection that makes him believe that my baby girl is his. Like the nigga is full-blown light skinned, and my baby is kissed by chocolate. Like, nothing is making sense.

I jump out of bed and catch a shower before I go over to my mom's to check in on her and my sister. As I am waiting for my breakfast, my mind shifts to Janet. While I have been in constant communication with Theodore, I can't begin to pretend to stomach her. Something isn't sitting well within my soul when it comes to her. Yeah, she adores Kynsley, but her smug looks are a bit to condescending. I don't think she will harm her; I just think her care and love—or lack thereof—is disingenuous.

If I'm being honest with myself, that is part of the reason Gaea and I connect on the level in which we did. The two people that are supposed to love and care for us and show us what an unconditional love is, they failed us. They give us our first heartbreaks that ultimately turn into scars, pushing us to a place where we crave love rather than healing. We're two broken souls, searching for healing in each other.

Once I knew for sure that Kynsley was mine, I made a vow to myself that she would never feel that type of pain. No kid deserves to go through life and search for the love of a parent. I make sure she feels the depth of my love in every ounce of any time we spend together. I put in not only my money but also my time because that's what she needs most. Knowing that she's missing when I never truly got the chance to be a father is crippling, and to top the shit off, Gaea is being so fucking stubborn. Once I have them both back in my life, I'm going to make it my life's mission to ensure that they're not only safe but also that Gaea knows what the fuck is up. I've had enough of her running when shit gets tough.

Armed with that feeling, I get out of bed, shower, and head toward my kitchen. Imagine my surprise when Tobias is not only in my kitchen but also in my home, eating my lunch. I'm not in the mood for his lectures today, but having someone around eases the sting of my girls not being with me.

"Hey, Kwame, I got a text earlier from Gaea, asking me to check out a Lisette Toussaint, and you may want to take a look at this," Tobias says, interrupting my thoughts.

"Aww, for real?" I ask, not really caring one way or another what the hell they were talking about. I try to play it cool, but I'm madder than a muthafucka. She's talking to every damn body in our circle but the one person she needs to talk to. I'm not with this passive aggressive shit, letting others know about shit before me. Hell, I'm her man. Well, am I? Man, fuck that. Ain't no guessing; I am her man.

"Stop being that way. You know you love the girl. She's just well... Simply put, she's Ana's sister."

"Ana's sister, huh? What's up with y'all anyway? Don't think I forgot about y'all coming back into the studio all discombobulated," I say, giving a half chuckle.

"Nothing. Mind ya business," he says, completely dismissing me. "But yo, I need you to take a look at what I found."

I walk over to take a look at his screen, and I'm

242

completely shocked at what I see. There is no way we could've missed this shit. I immediately pick up my phone and dial Theodore.

"Hey, Pops, I need you to check something out," I blurt out.

"Are you speaking about this Lisette Toussaint that Gaea sent over?" he asks. "I have a file about two inches thick, but I haven't been able to look at it quite yet."

"We went to undergrad with her. But I don't see how she would connect with Kynsley."

"Hmm…" he says while shuffling through some papers. "It looks as if the connection just so happens to be none other than Aaron W. Williamson."

Gaea's dad, Tobias, and I decide that instead of having this conversation over the phone, it will be best if we had this conversation face to face. We agree upon a time to meet, but I also decide that with recent events, despite how pissed off I am at Gaea, I need her safe. I've been kicking myself ever since I walked out the door on her. It was childish, but my feelings were 100 percent valid. Yes, I understand her viewpoint on Maxwell being a suspect, but she isn't even willing to explore the possibility that there are other avenues. Hell, that's my father, and while I don't want to believe it, I threw his ass in the list of people to look out for. Why? Because the love of my daughter won't allow me to just let anyone to be overlooked. If I thought it was my mother, I would have thrown her in the list of people I thought wanted to hurt Kynsley.

Armed with this information, I make my way over to Gaea's house to sit down and have an actual conversation—one that requires us to put our differences aside and to focus on facts rather than emotions. While I love this woman, it's her stubbornness that I can only stomach in small doses. I can't shake this spine-chilling feeling as I turn to get on the off ramp toward her house. Not wanting to alert Pops on just a feeling, I call Tobias up and ask him, along with security, to meet me at the house.

As I pull into her driveway, nothing appears to be out of place. Her purple Jeep Wrangler Sahara sits in her driveway as normal, and her landscaping looks beautiful as it always has. But once I get to the door, my heart drops into my stomach. The bright-yellow door is left slightly ajar. I don't get a good feeling by the door being open. She never leaves doors open despite her living in a gated community. Sensing she may be in some kind of trouble I forego waiting on security and calling the police. I rush into the house with wild abandon, searching the house and frantically calling out to her. By the time I make it to her bedroom, I hear footsteps and more voices. I take it as my cue that security and the police Tobias had called finally made it.

I enter her bedroom and feel a sense of relief when I see her curled in bed, fast asleep. She looks so peaceful and angelic in that moment that I don't want to disturb her. In this moment, I know I can't live without her. But I won't reveal that fact to her until I know she is on the same page as me romantically, physically, and spiritually. I'm not in the space to properly deal with my feelings and she's definitely not in the space to accept what I had to offer her. I gently stir her to get her to open those eyes I've come to love.

"Hey, Gypsy. Wake up, baby," I speak gently, and she starts to move. She looks shocked to see me as she opens her eyes. Then I see a flicker in her eyes and know that whatever is about to come out of her mouth is about to be some straight bullshit. But I'd rather hear that than to not hear anything at all. Her time to tame that mouth will soon come of that, I'm sure.

"I see showing up unannounced seems to be a strong point of yours. But let me also add breaking and entering to that list," she says, rolling her eyes and moving out of my grasp. I make the choice to ignore her stubborn ass. Now knowing that she's safe, I start to move around the room, packing her bags.

"I didn't break in, Gaea. The door was open. Get out of the bed and start helping me to pack these bags so we can go. Better yet, throw some clothes on, and I'll pay someone to come pack up the house."

"Have you lost your mind? My door was closed. I made sure I locked up and set the alarm prior to lying down for a nap. Furthermore, I am not giving up my house to live with you."

"First, you have no choice in the matter anymore. The door was not only unlocked, but it was also opened. But your so-called alarm system was disarmed. Now get up willingly, or be moved forcefully," I declare. Getting the feel that I'm dead serious, she gets up and collects her things. Once she's gathered most of the things she thinks she'll need, we make our way to the door.

"Aye, Flash, I need you to come check something out," Kion, the head of my security, says, and the look on his face lets me know it's something he doesn't want Gaea to see. I instruct Tobias to stay put with Gaea until I check out what they've found. She objects and follows me despite my better judgement. It seems like a lifetime flashes amongst us before we make the trek to Kynsley's room.

I make the decision to open the door and immediately regret the choice. Gaea, let's out a gut-wrenching scream as I lose the contents of my stomach on the floor. The room is completely destroyed. The curtains are ripped down. Toys are broken, and a ripped picture of Kynsley and Gaea has a knife with a snake attached to it stuck in the wall. But what gets me is a filthy image of my baby on the bed.

Smeared across her wall is a bloody message:

YOU RUINED MY LIFE THREE YEARS AGO AND FOR THAT YOU MUST PAY! CALL OFF THE COPS OR SIX FEET UNDER SHALL YOUR DAUGHTER LAY!

Dear Reader,

First, if you are reading this page, I thank you. I thank you for taking a chance on a new author. I hope to be one that you enjoy and that you give me a chance to enter your heart for a while. Like most of you, I am an avid reader myself, so I will get your frustration with me. But bear with me, for I am human. Although I welcome all constructive criticism, please allow me the chance to process it before I respond, for I am a thinker. I will say that if you're looking for a novel with a reformed thug or a man strictly from the streets, this is not the novel for you. Will I eventually write one? Who knows? I'll follow wherever my pen leads me. I hope you enjoy my first baby as much as I enjoyed writing it. Please leave an honest review. I would greatly and graciously appreciate it.

Peace and blessings,

brittjoni

-PENNING LOVE NATURALLY-

Be sure to LIKE our Major Key

Publishing page on Facebook!

CPSIA information can be obtained
at www.ICGtesting.com
Printed in the USA
LVHW05s0046120418
573117LV00020BC/271/P